The beautiful Miss Camilla Marsh has been groomed from childhood for her marriage to Javier da Silva Ballantyne, the aristocratic owner of a tea plantation in Ceylon. Yet when she travels there in 1877 to marry the man she has never seen, her romantic dreams are shattered.

The estate at Ratnagalla is a paradise, but there are undercurrents threatening to make Camilla's life there intolerable—particularly as her new husband obviously considers their marriage merely as a business arrangement.

Will Camilla let Javier's stony indifference drive her back to England? Or will she stay to fight for the man she loves, the destiny she believes is theirs and the place towards which she feels all her life has been leading her?

Honeymoon
in Ceylon

Lee Stafford

MILLS & BOON LIMITED
London · Sydney · Toronto

First published in Great Britain 1982
by Mills & Boon Limited, 15–16 Brook's Mews,
London W1A 1DR

ISBN 0 263 74113 3

04/0183

Set in 10 on 11 pt Times Roman

*Photoset by Rowland Phototypesetting Ltd
Bury St Edmunds, Suffolk
Made and printed in Great Britain by
Cox & Wyman Ltd, Reading*

CHAPTER
ONE

ONE morning in February of 1877, a young woman stood on the deck of the ship which had brought her from England and gazed out over the calm, almost land-locked waters of Colombo harbour. The merest hint of a breeze ruffled her silvery-fair, upswept curls, and the vessels riding at bay seemed painted on a motionless background of blue.

She herself was hardly less still, and was only half aware of the scene before her. Even though Ceylon was new to her, and would, from today, be her home, she was too deeply involved in her own thoughts to pay it much attention. Her calm demeanour and the composed expression of her precise, almost classical features, concealed a mounting excitement that was tinged, not unnaturally, with apprehension. Any moment now he would appear, and she would meet the man she had travelled thousands of miles to marry.

It seemed to Camilla that she had been groomed from childhood for marriage to Javier da Silva Ballantyne. Her knowledge of his existence stretched back as far as she could remember into her childhood, and her awareness of their twin destinies almost as far. When she was very young he was, to her, like the prince of a distant country. Everything about him appeared clothed in romance, even his name, a legacy of his English father and Portuguese mother, and he lived in a land whose very name breathed exotic scents and spices. Ceylon. The ancient kingdom whose Sanskrit name, Sri Lanka, meant 'the resplendent land'.

Camilla's mother had died when she was born, and her father, a wealthy industrialist, was killed in a hunting accident when she was still very small; consequently she remembered neither of them. She had been brought up by her maternal grandparents, Colonel and Lady Sumter, whose adored only grandchild she was.

Childhood, to Camilla, had meant India. Her grandfather's regiment was stationed first in Assam and Bengal, later in Madras, and she grew up watched over by soft-voiced Indian ayahs, speaking Bengali and Tamil as easily as English. India was home, it was the natural place to be, and she wept bitter tears when her grandmother gently told her that now she was a big girl she would have to be sent to school in England. And it was then that Lady Sumter had confided to the grave-faced, serious child, her hopes for her future.

'You know, your grandfather has told you many times, the story of how he met Edgar Ballantyne on the ship coming out from England, long ago.'

'Yes, I know. Grandfather was returning from leave, and Mr Ballantyne was coming out to India with the intention of planting tea and becoming rich.' Camilla knew the story off by heart. Edgar Ballantyne was a younger son with not much money, but a great store of determination. The ideal of getting rich in India strode hand in hand with the tradition of civil and military service, through the pages of history, and he was coming East, as generations of young Englishmen had, to make his fortune. To the middle-aged officer and his wife, who had left *their* only daughter at school in England, this venturesome young man who had dash, and style, and a drive to succeed, was like a surrogate son. The friendship endured as the officer climbed the ladder of promotion to Colonel, and the young man became a successful planter. Once, when climatic conditions threatened to ruin Ballantyne's venture, it was Colonel Sumter who loaned him the money to see him through.

He repaid not only the cash, but the debt of honour, by saving the Colonel's life during a hunting expedition they shared.

An adventurous spirit had taken young Ballantyne on to Ceylon, where he acquired a Portuguese heiress as his wife, and bought a coffee plantation known as Ratna-galla. There he had settled, happily transplanted like the young tea bushes with which he began to experiment, convinced that the crop he had grown in Assam could flourish on the island, although at the time coffee was king. The other planters laughed at his ambitions, and he gained a reputation for eccentricity.

'And then Javier was born,' Camilla concluded the tale triumphantly. 'Some years later, I was born. And in all these years, we have never met.'

'No,' her grandmother admitted, 'but we kept in touch. Such closeness cannot be diminished by distance. We heard when Javier's younger brother and sister were born. And we always hoped that one day, our families would be united. By marriage, my dear—yours and Javier's.'

Camilla had drawn in her breath.

'Then I would live in Ceylon, and never have to be sent away again, and one day, when grandfather retires from the army, you could come and live with us. We could all be together.'

Her grandmother had smiled. 'A nice thought, but that is all in the future. In the meantime, what kind of a wife would you be for any man if you are not suitably educated, do not have all the accomplishments a lady should have, do not know how to mix with the best society? That is why you must go to England, my dear, although heaven knows, we shall miss you terribly.'

In the first lonely years of her life at boarding school, homesick for the sights and smells and textures of her childhood home, and appalled by this cold and unfriend-ly land to which she had been sent, Camilla would lie in bed at night and weave dreams about Javier, how he would rescue her from her unhappiness, and take her back to a land where it was always warm, and the sun shone. In time, of course, she settled down, made friends, and applied herself to her studies, but in her deepest self she never thought of her sojourn in England as anything but temporary. Her real life was back there, waiting for her.

At the age of eighteen, Camilla left school and 'came out'. Hitherto, she had spent her vacations at the homes of friends, but for this momentous occasion Lady Sumter returned to England to give Camilla her season, although her husband was unable to accompany her. Camilla was presented at court and launched in society. She had beauty and élan, and as her father's sole heir she was also immensely rich. Not surprisingly, she was a sensation. There were balls and parties, and coveys of young men clamouring to escort her, to dance with her, and to lavish her with attention.

All this was mildly enjoyable, but Camilla did not let it go to her head. She knew she was attractive, she had only to look in the mirror to see the slim but shapely figure, the ivory skin and chiselled features, the masses of silvery blonde hair. That she was wealthy did not so readily occur to her. The money left to her by her father was held in trust by her grandparents, and they had always lived comfortably but modestly, so for the most part she never gave it a thought. If there were fortune hunters, as there undoubtedly were, they did not get very far with Camilla, nor did she evince interest in any of the young men who languished around her. She thought of herself as already promised, although she did not speak of it to anyone.

'But when are we going home?' she asked her grandmother one evening, as she was getting ready for another ball.

'My dear child, aren't you enjoying your season?'

'Of course, and I'm grateful to you for coming all this way and leaving grandfather for so long to give it to me.' Camilla looked at her grandmother, and her affection was touched by concern. Lady Sumter was getting old, she realised. She had arthritis, and was finding it increasingly difficult to get about. 'I'm longing to see grandfather again, and to be back in India. It seems such ages since we were all there.'

'You must see Europe while you have the chance,' her grandmother admonished. 'I know this new Suez canal has made the journey much easier, but it is still a long way, and trips to Europe will be few and far between for a busy planter's wife. Oh, yes.' She saw her granddaughter's eyes light up. 'We had a letter from Edgar shortly before I left, and his hopes, and ours, are still the same.'

Buoyed up by this hope, Camilla did a grand tour of Europe, accompanied by an old schoolfriend and her parents. She saw Paris and Rome and Venice, she crossed the Alps and marvelled at the majestic beauty of Switzerland, she waltzed in Vienna and drank wine in small cafés in the Wienerwald. She loved every minute of it, but it was all in the nature of a picture show. It did not sadden her to think that she might not see it again until she brought her own daughters to enjoy the same experience.

Finally back in England, she was overjoyed to learn that her grandmother was at last making plans for a return to Madras. They spent hours poring over catalogues and choosing suitable clothes for Camilla, almost as if, the girl thought excitedly, they were buying her trousseau.

'We shall invite Javier to visit us in Madras, if his father can spare him from the plantation,' Lady Sumter announced, in a tone which said she did not, in this instance, expect a refusal.

Suddenly nervous, Camilla had said, 'What if he doesn't like me?'

'My dear, you are so lovely he could hardly fail to like you,' the old lady said. 'But remember, Camilla—marriage is not moonshine and nonsense. It is two people working together for a common good. For a woman, that means constant sacrifice for her husband, and then her children's interests.'

'Surely, her sacrifice is recompensed by love?' the girl said impulsively.

'If she is fortunate,' her grandmother said equably. 'You see, Camilla, it is not always possible to experience what you call "love" before marriage. Flights of fancy, which could easily be mistaken, are what the young generally confuse with abiding passion. Love more often comes from living with a man, bearing his children, facing together all the perils and problems that arise.'

She looked down at Camilla's blonde head, and went on, quietly, 'You are not just any girl, to be permitted to throw herself away on just any young man. On your mother's side, you come of an old and respected family, with a long tradition of service to India. From your father, you will inherit immense wealth when you marry, and we must avoid fortune hunters whose only care is to get their hands on your money. The Ballantynes do not need your money, although put together with their own it will be a force to reckon with. Javier is wealthy enough in his own right. This will not be simply a marriage, Camilla. You will be founding a dynasty.'

She could not but be impressed by her grandmother's steady conviction. But was it wrong to nurse her own romantic dream, to feel, secretly and instinctively, that Javier was her destiny, and she his? That she would love him from the beginning?

That afternoon was mild and pleasant, so Camilla had her horse saddled up and went for a brisk ride across the fields. She returned, her cheeks glowing from the exercise, full of a happy anticipation of all that lay ahead, and walked, totally without premonition, into a hushed and yet strangely disturbed house. The sense of something wrong was palpable, even as she stood in the hall, and she frowned. Slim and straight in her mulberry-coloured riding habit, trimmed with grey, she paused, aware all at once that her life had reached a sudden and unexpected watershed.

'Oh, Miss Camilla!'

Her grandmother's maid, Fanny, a strong, reed-thin, middle-aged woman who had been with Lady Sumter for years, and was totally reliable, came swiftly down the stairs towards her.

'What is it, Fanny? What's happened?' Camilla asked urgently.

'The doctor's here, Miss, he'll be out to speak to you in just a minute.' Fanny took Camilla's hat and gloves, and propelled the girl towards the drawing-room with the familiarity of long service. 'I'll ring for some tea, shall I?'

'Tea? It's a little early for tea, Fanny,' Camilla said mechanically, her mind on the rest of what the maid had said. 'Why is the doctor here? My grandmother was well this morning—her legs were troubling her, but no more than usual.'

'It's the shock, Miss—oh, here's Dr Bates, now.' Fanny was anxious to be off upstairs to Lady Sumter, and Camilla and the doctor were left facing each other across the drawing room.

Dr Bates was not a young man, in fact he was on the verge of retirement. He had attended the family, whenever they were in England, for many years, and it was he who had brought Camilla into the world. It had always been his regret that in spite of all his endeavours he had been unable to save her mother, and now it was his unpleasant duty to tell this lovely girl the worst news she had ever received in her sheltered young life.

'It's your grandfather,' he said. 'A wire came whilst you were out riding. My dear, there's no way to spare you this, or make it easier for you. He's dead.'

Camilla sank slowly onto a chair. She was too numb for grief, and was grateful for the arrival of the tea, which gave her something to do with her hands. The ritual completed, she was able to ask, in tones which the old doctor privately considered too steady for her own good, 'How did it happen?'

'It was his heart, apparently—very sudden, and comparatively painless, I would imagine,' he said, trying to offer some comfort. 'Your grandmother was deeply shocked, as you would expect. I have given her a sedative, and she will sleep for some time, but when she comes round she is going to need you. As you know, her own health is not good.'

'Of course.' Mechanically, Camilla sipped the tea, scarcely tasting the hot liquid. She herself had not yet accepted fully that her beloved grandfather was dead, that after being away from him for so many years she would never see him again.

After the doctor had left, Camilla went upstairs and sat beside Lady Sumter's bed. The blinds were drawn, and the room gradually darkened, and still Camilla sat, refusing to move, insisting that she be there when her grandmother awoke, condescending only to pick at the food Fanny had sent up on a tray.

It was late when the still figure on the bed finally stirred, and the old lady's thin hand reached out to clasp Camilla's warm young one. She remembered what the doctor had said, her grandmother would need her, but she could not help it, her own grief was suddenly released, and tears were running down her cheeks. Kneeling beside the bed, she laid her head on the coverlet and wept, and paradoxically, comforting the girl seemed to give Lady Sumter a new infusion of strength.

'If you hadn't been here with me, if you had been with him, it might never have happened,' Camilla gulped, and her grandmother shook her head.

'No, my dear, it could have happened at any time. Your grandfather has had a heart condition for several years, and successfully hid the fact from everyone but me. He wouldn't have told me either, but you can't live with someone as long as I have lived with him and not know when something is amiss. But he insisted you were not told, that nothing should spoil this time for you.'

'We should have gone back sooner. All these balls and parties, and gallivanting around Europe—I could have done without it.'

'Now, Camilla. A girl has to be properly launched in society, and we should have failed in our duty if we hadn't done so. There is still your future to consider.'

At that time, Camilla was too upset to be thinking seriously about her future. But as the months passed communications arrived from Ceylon, and events began to move in a way she could not ignore.

Colonel Sumter's will had expressly stated that his body was not to be shipped home to England, and he had been buried in India, where he had served for so long. With his death, the ties that had bound the family to that country were severed, there was no son or grandson to join the regiment. There was only Camilla, and her grandfather's last testament indicated clearly what he wanted for her.

It seemed by some strange quirk of fate that his death had been a dual tragedy, and that even in death the Sumters and the Ballantynes were joined. For what had brought on that fatal heart attack had been the shock of hearing that Edgar Ballantyne, whom he had befriended as a young man so long ago, had died. His last wish had been for the marriage of his elder son, Javier, to the granddaughter of Colonel and Lady Sumter, stated the letter from his widow, Doña Lucia.

With the letter came a small, well-wrapped package, which, when opened, revealed an exquisite necklet of milky pearls.

Lady Sumter fingered them carefully, and looked long and steadily at Camilla.

'This is a formal request for your hand in marriage,' she said. 'These pearls are an heirloom of Doña Lucia's family. If you wear them, you are to consider yourself betrothed to Javier.'

Camilla hesitated.

'I wonder why he does not write to me himself,' she said. 'Is it a Portuguese custom to become engaged by proxy?'

Lady Sumter smiled.

'The circumstances are somewhat difficult. If we were living in Madras, or if his father were still alive, no doubt he would come in person to give you the necklace. But his mother writes that he now has the full responsibility of running the tea estate, and cannot possibly leave it to come to England. They wish you to go to Ceylon and be married there.'

Camilla's heart began to beat faster.

'For me to go . . . but I . . . but we have never met! Furthermore, you are not well enough for such a journey, and I cannot leave you.'

Lady Sumter's eyes were knowing as she regarded the flustered girl.

'Child, you know that this marriage is what we have always planned, always wanted for you. But if you are unwilling, you must not feel you are obliged to go through with it. However, you are not to use my health for an excuse. It is true that I cannot get about very well, and that I could not stand a long voyage, but I am not in my dotage. I have all that I need here for the time that is left to me, and I should spend that time more comfortably if I knew you were settled in your own home with a good husband, not on the loose here, a prey to every man who would like to get his hands on your money after I am gone.'

She took Camilla's inert hand, and folded it gently around the pearl necklace.

'Now, I suggest you go up to your room and spend some time in constructive thought,' she said. 'Decide what you truly want, Camilla, and when you are sure, one way or the other, we shall write to Doña Lucia with your answer.'

Camilla sat for a long time at her bedroom window, gazing out and seeing little. She thought of all the years when she had dreamed of marriage to Javier, all the years when she had accepted as natural that it would take place. She thought of her grandfather, whose dearest wish it had been, and of Edgar Ballantyne, whom she had never known, who had shared that dream. She saw her life, and Javier's, running like two curves, separate but concurrent, and predestined eventually to converge. And finally she listened to her heart, to the tug of the East, the inescapable draw which was in her blood. Ceylon. Sri Lanka. The resplendent land. Across the oceans, its magnetism reached out and touched her, telling her that the man who awaited her there was right for her, telling her that she was going home.

When she came down to dinner that evening, her grandmother was gratified to note that around her neck, Camilla was wearing the da Silva pearls.

Much of this was going through Camilla's mind as she gazed out from the deck of the ship. Below, in her cabin, she knew that Fanny was organising her luggage—dear, capable Fanny, whom her grandmother had insisted must accompany her to her new home. For Camilla it was a brief moment alone, to reflect on the old life before embarking upon the new. So wrapped up in this contemplation was she, that it startled her when the steward appeared at her elbow.

'Excuse me, Miss, but there's a gentleman come aboard looking for you.'

Camilla jumped, and turned abruptly. He was here—

and she had been so deep in thought she had never even seen him come on board. The moment which should have been so significant had been allowed to creep up stealthily on her, like a thief. She steadied herself, took a deep breath and smiled, regaining at least the outward appearance of composure.

'Miss Marsh? Miss Camilla Marsh?'

The young man who bowed over her hand was tall, with a kind of indolent grace. His skin was tanned, as was that of all men in the tropics by constant exposure to the sun, but only lightly, it was not the weatherbeaten darkness she remembered of men's faces in Madras. His hair was bronze, tending to auburn—the Ballantynes all had a red streak and a temper to match it, she had once heard her grandfather remark—and his eyes were greyish blue. His white tropical suit was immaculate, and his hands as smooth and cared for as hers, and all in all, he looked more like one of the leisured young men who made a business of attending as many social events as they could crush into their schedule, than a hardworking plantation owner.

He was smiling down at her with a kind of mocking, playful admiration, and deep inside her Camilla felt an unaccountable sinking of the spirit. She did not know how to describe the sudden depression of her emotions, or exactly what caused it, for she had spent only a few moments in this man's company. But she knew, instinctively, that this was someone she could perhaps find amusing, could like, could possibly sympathise with, but not a man she could respect. She had carried in her mind for so long a mental picture of Javier Ballantyne, a picture which consisted not merely of physical characteristics—indeed, these were only vaguely included. Rather, it was an aura of personality, of the many facets which, together, comprised the uniqueness of any human being. And the man who stood before her now was at variance with that picture.

'Mr Ballantyne?' She kept her voice as calm as possible. Her grandmother had warned her against moonshine and nonsense, and she had no right to be disappointed because he did not live up to some shadowy romantic image.

'That's right,' he said cheerfully. 'Phillip Ballantyne, to be precise. A pleasure to make your acquaintance. Did you have a good voyage?'

Camilla's hazel eyes opened wider. *Phillip* Ballantyne? She stood perfectly still for a moment, while her questioning senses subsided.

'You're not Javier?'

'Absolutely not,' he agreed, unperturbed. 'I say . . . did you think I was?'

'How would I know, Mr Ballantyne, since I have never met either of you before?' she replied gravely. 'I only knew I would be met off the ship at Colombo, and naturally, I assumed . . .' her voice tailed off, leaving him to work out for himself what she had assumed, which he did with alacrity.

'You assumed that the lucky bridegroom would be here to meet his bride in person?' He laughed. 'You don't know my brother, Miss Marsh. It is my sad duty to inform you that you have a very demanding rival— several hundred acres of prime tea country.'

Camilla favoured him with the ice-cool, stony gaze she had inherited from Lady Sumter. It was enough that she had travelled so many miles alone with her maid to marry this young man's brother only to find that he was not sufficiently enthusiastic about her arrival to meet the ship in person. She was not obliged also to suffer Phillip Ballantyne's flippant attitude.

'I find your manner a trifle offensive, sir,' she said coldly.

He was instant contrition—a little too instant for sincerity, Camilla could not help reflecting.

'Oh, I say—I do apologise. It's an effect I seem to have

on people, quite unintentionally,' he said. 'What I meant was, if you were going to marry me, I would certainly have been here to meet you.'

The suggestion of a smile played around Camilla's lips. She was fairly certain that his ingenuous manner was faked, that he knew only too well how his comments would be received. All the same, it was difficult not to be amused.

'But you *are* here, Mr Ballantyne,' she pointed out.

'So I am,' he agreed, with a wide smile. 'My brother, of course, sends his apologies, and regrets it is not possible at present for him to undertake a journey that involves several days away from the estate. He's desperately busy. My time, of course, isn't worth very much, and can therefore be discounted.'

This last remark was delivered with a light, throwaway sarcasm, and Camilla inquired curiously, 'Oh? You do not then help your brother on the plan . . . that is, the estate?'

He laughed.

'Fieldwork is not much in my line, Miss Marsh. I can just about distinguish one crop from another, but that's as deep as my knowledge goes. Nor do I have a head for business. I'm what's known as a dead loss. My contribution consists mostly of running the old errand from time to time, particularly if it necessitates a trip to Colombo.'

The odd errand, such as escorting a prospective bride, Camilla thought, her lips tightening. But there was nothing for it but to put herself and her luggage into the hands of Phillip Ballantyne, who was busy informing her that the first part of their journey would be by train to Nuwara Eliya, and that since the building of the railroad, going up country had become a far less hazardous and tiring prospect.

Once in the comfort of the railway carriage, Camilla was able to relax a little, and was soon so entranced by the scene unfolding before her that she forgot Phillip and his slightly facetious manner, forgot—almost—her disappointment that Javier himself had not come to meet her. Ceylon was all around her, welcoming her with its beauty and diversity, and the spell of its fascination laid immediate fingers on her soul.

There were brief glimpses of palm-fringed beaches and lagoons, broken by rocky headlands, before their route turned inland, through a world where streams meandered lazily through the tender green of the rice fields. Slowly, they began to climb into the hills, undulating at first, and then ever more steep, into a different world, fold upon fold of blue mountains rising into the distance, bridges spanning spectacular gorges and ravines, where waterfalls cascaded theatrically, filling the air with clouds of spray through which the sunlight danced and sparkled. They passed villages of wattle-and-daub houses, thatched with coconut palm or straw, and here and there, caught glimpses of impressive granite bungalows set amidst splendid lawns and gardens.

Many of the slopes were heavily planted with a crop bearing dark, glossy green leaves that Phillip told her was coffee, which had been for some time the island's mainstay. Some of these trees looked healthy and productive, but others were clearly diseased, their leaves blighted with rust-coloured spots and a thick, powdery yellow substance which gave the entire field an unhealthy appearance. And they passed some places where wholesale clearing and uprooting was taking place, leaving only the blasted stumps.

'But what's wrong with the trees?' Camilla cried out, horrified by the sight.

Phillip shrugged carelessly.

'Coffee blight,' he said. 'It's spreading through the coffee plantations at a tremendous rate. Many of these fellows have started to panic and sell up. Not a few have been ruined. Those who had the cash, or the foresight, have begun to replace it with tea.'

'As you have?'

'Yes, our father was one of the pioneers of tea planting in Ceylon. He always grew tea, although only experimentally at first, so we were ready to make the changeover more speedily than most. Mad Ballantyne, some of the other planters called him. But he had the last laugh.'

His son laughed, too, a hard, humourless laughter, which bore not a trace of pity for the ruined coffee planters. Camilla glanced sidelong at this strange young man for a moment, wondering at the depth of embitterment in one so youthful, then she gave her full attention back to the splendour of the scenery.

Nuwara Eliya, the City of Lights, was primarily known as a health resort amongst the European residents of Ceylon, but arriving after dark Camilla saw little of it. She was glad, however, of the civilised comforts of the hotel where it had been arranged that they should stay, and the prospect of a hot bath and a good night's rest. Tomorrow, Phillip had told her, they continued their journey on horseback. The railway system was still in its infancy and only served a few of the planting districts, and the Ballantyne estate was, as he somewhat distastefully expressed it, 'confoundedly remote'.

She had agreed with her future brother-in-law that it might be better if she had dinner sent to her room. In the dining-room, who knew what acquaintances might be encountered? In so small and closed a society everyone knew everyone else, and there would be much speculation about the strange young woman dining with the younger Ballantyne. Camilla did not feel ready to face a barrage of questioning glances and whispered comments. If Javier had been with her, and able to introduce her as 'my fiancée', she might well have summoned up sufficient nerve, but reduced to the status of a parcel to be collected from the docks, she lacked this confidence.

As for Phillip, he undoubtedly had fish of his own to fry, and seemed quite relieved to be free of his responsibility towards her for a while. Well—he was young, personable, and single, Camilla thought tolerantly. There must be pleasanter ways for him to pass the evening than entertaining the girl who was to marry his brother.

Fanny had maintained a tight-lipped silence as she saw to Camilla's bath, brushed out her hair and arranged to have her riding habit pressed ready for the next day. It would have been difficult for Camilla not to have sensed her disapproval, which had become noticeable on her first acquaintance with Phillip Ballantyne.

'You don't like him very much, do you, Fanny?' she asked.

The older woman continued to brush her young mistresses hair with long, regular strokes.

'He's likeable enough, Miss, but I wouldn't trust him,' she answered soberly. 'I remember his father, just a little, although I was only a young girl at the time. He could charm birds out of the trees, and any woman he'd a mind to, but there was a wildness underneath it, if you see what I mean.'

Pausing with the brush in her hand, she seemed to be gazing back into the past, as she continued, less critically.

'Mr Edgar—we always knew him as Mr Edgar, because he was more like a son to the Colonel—he was a worker, no doubt about that. He set his mind to doing something and he did it. If he wanted something he always got it in the end, and it wasn't by luck. I suppose a man has to have a bit of adventure in his soul, to come out East and make his way like that. But this young gentleman—' she sniffed disdainfully—'the wildness may be there, but I doubt if he's done a day's work in his life.'

Camilla listened thoughtfully. It was not considered

proper for a servant to criticise those whom society deemed her betters, but Fanny, secure in her long years of service to Lady Sumter, and her fierce, protective interest in what was best for 'her' family, felt free to dispense with propriety when she thought it necessary, and Camilla valued her frankness.

'Fortunately, I'm not marrying Mr Phillip Ballantyne,' she reminded her maid, with a hint of a twinkle in her eye.

Fanny pursed her thin lips, and shook her head.

'And who knows but what his brother has the wildness, too,' she muttered darkly.

Camilla smiled gently.

'It would appear Javier cannot win your approval, whatever he does,' she pointed out mildly. 'You disapprove of him because he did not come to meet me in person, and if he had, you would have branded him a wastrel for neglecting his duties on the estate.'

'It's not for me to approve or otherwise,' Fanny said primly, notwithstanding the fact that this was exactly what she had been doing. 'And anyway, Miss, I prefer to reserve judgment until I've met the gentleman.'

Camilla could not resist a chuckle at these two contradictory statements, but Fanny's eyes were serious and, slowly, she said, 'You don't think this marriage is a good idea, do you, Fanny?'

The maid set down the brush, and began to busy herself putting away the clothes Camilla had travelled in.

'I think the world of your grandmother, and I respect her decisions, because they usually turn out to be right,' she said. 'But oh, Miss Camilla, aren't there hundreds of nice young men in England, without your having to come all this way to marry one you don't even know?'

Camilla gave this question her full and serious consideration.

'Maybe there are. And maybe a few of them are rich

enough not to be after my money. But, Fanny—perhaps I, too, have adventure in my soul.'

'Perhaps you'll need it, Miss,' Fanny said gravely, and on that sobering thought, Camilla slept.

They set out next morning in brilliant sunshine. The air was bright and sparkling, like an English summer day, but with that crisp, invigorating bite peculiar to hill country. The last traces of habitation were soon behind them, and they were riding ever deeper into the hills. Beyond each ridge they crested stretched ever more convolutions, rising steeply to jagged peaks that seemed to touch the intense blue of the sky. The bright green of the tea estates with their disciplined rows and terraces of bushes contrasted strongly with the untamed grandeur of the high peaks, culminating in the splendour of Adam's Peak, which broke the skyline to the north.

Here and there they heard the ring of axes as trees were felled, clearing more space for planting, and patient, lumbering elephants did the heavy work of moving the debris. Here, nimble-fingered workers, men and women, moved along the rows, skilfully plucking the young tips of the shoots. The heat and skin-drenching humidity, the noise and bustle of Colombo might never have existed, for this was another world, a world of eternal spring. Camilla felt her heart lifting, her spirits grow lighter. How could she fail to be happy here?

They had lunch at a pleasant rest-house which might almost have been an English inn, and then set off again, traversing a long valley hemmed in by hills on both sides. Here they saw no more estates of tea or coffee, no signs of human habitation, the silence was broken only by the cries of birds, and their own voices. For the best part of the afternoon they rode, resting occasionally, and still there was nothing to indicate that anyone lived, worked and planted crops among these beautiful, unending hills.

They came out at last on to a high plateau, with stupendous vistas of mountain peaks in the distance, and then descended to 5,000 feet, following the valley of a sizeable river. There was a neat Sinhalese village, with every house surrounded by lush gardens full of flowers and vegetables, some growing coffee of their own. From a temple, a benign, all-knowing Buddha watched their progress without surprise, and dark-eyed children with the pale olive complexions of the Sinhalese regarded them with more curiosity.

'What a charming village,' Camilla remarked, impressed by the generally clean and prosperous appearance.

Phillip Ballantyne gave a snort of disapproval.

'Charming maybe, the Sinhalese are that, but they're idle devils, and won't work on the estates. As long as they have their bits of land, producing enough for them to live on, they won't stir themselves to do more. Consequently, we have to go to the trouble and expense of importing Tamil labour from India, which we then have to house and support.'

Camilla could see his point, but against all the ethics of her time she could see that it might be pleasant to live in the neat, sunlit village, growing enough food for one's family, and conceded that the villagers might have good reason not to want to exchange that life for the hard graft of work on someone else's land. She supposed if her father had thought in like manner she would not now be heir to such vast wealth, but nonetheless, she saw that the question was not as one-sided as it appeared to Phillip—and no doubt, to most of the planting fraternity.

Now, once again, the tea country was all around them in neat, ordered terraces, stretching up and down hillsides as far as the eye could see.

'Almost there,' Phillip said cheerfully. 'Round the

next bend, and you can see the bungalow. What a time to arrive—too late for afternoon tea, and too early for a brandy and soda!'

The energy demanded by the long ride, and the sheer fascination of the country had fully occupied Camilla's mind hitherto, but now, suddenly, she was nervous. She felt her breath fluttering and her heart thumping uncomfortably in her chest, and she was conscious of an honest, cowardly impulse to turn and ride back through the rows of young trees, through the village and down the long valley. It was a fierce impulse, strongly felt, but she never seriously considered giving in to it, and not merely because, alone, she would very soon be lost and helpless.

No, she had come here as part of a covenant, and where could she go where she would not know that she had broken her side of the agreement? The pioneering spirit of her long Anglo-Indian heritage came to her rescue. She compressed her lips firmly and rode forward, towards her future home.

During the long day's ride Phillip had chatted to Camilla, to pass the time, and because he was of an obviously gregarious nature, with an eye for a pretty girl. Much of what he said was inconsequential gossip about people Camilla did not know, but now and again he would toss out a remark about his family, which she would grasp eagerly and mentally file away.

'You'll find us a strange lot up at Ratnagalla,' he had warned her. 'We're a pretty mixed bag, anyway, and you can deduce a lot from the way we each of us prefer to be known. My mother, for instance, styles herself Doña Lucia Ballantyne da Silva, as if the fact of marrying my father was not to be permitted to encroach on her aristocratic Portuguese lineage.'

He grimaced. 'My brother strikes a nice balance between the two, and calls himself Javier da Silva Ballantyne, which indicates that he accepts both sides of our

racial inheritance. As for me,' he continued flippantly,
'I'm plain Phillip Ballantyne to everyone who knows me.
And my sister, Helen, is anxious only to be rid of her
name altogether, and take someone else's.'

A strange lot indeed, Camilla mused, preparing herself inwardly for her first meeting with her new family. A
facetious brother-in-law who wanted only to be an English gentleman of leisure, a mother-in-law who clung to
her Portuguese heritage, and a sister-in-law who was
interested only in marriage! And what of Javier himself?
Was she to infer from what his brother had said that in
him the two strains had blended and lived together in
harmony?

Round the next bend and you can see the bungalow,
he had said, and now, indeed, Camilla could see it. She
had passed many similar homes on the way up through
the hill country, so she was not misled by the word
'bungalow' into expecting anything small and cosy. Her
new home was a large, two-storeyed stone built house
with steep gables at either end, set on a slight elevation
which caused one to approach it by a broad, stepped
path through a series of terraced lawns, the topmost one
neatly balustraded. The windows winked diamond
bright in the sun, the lawns were verdantly green and
manicured to perfection, bordered by masses of flowers
—larkspurs, pansies, sweet william, dahlias. English
flowers, but finer and more colourful than any Camilla
had seen in England. And everywhere, roses, magnificent roses of every possible hue and variety, growing in
splendid profusion. A covered verandah ran the full
length of the bungalow's frontage, and here there were
cane reclining chairs, tables, and yet more roses, planted
in stone tubs and urns.

'Well—what do you think?' said Phillip, helping
Camilla to dismount, and giving the horses into the care
of a servant, who had instantly materialised, in the way
common to all well-run households.

'It's a perfect site,' murmured Camilla, 'and the finest garden I have ever seen.'

'Ah, that's my mother's province, she adores her roses. Nature helps, of course. Just about everything grows here. Shall we go in?'

He offered Camilla his arm and they ascended the serried rows of steps between the lawns, Fanny following behind with Camilla's valise. Her hand on his sleeve was steady, her step firm, and only the tightening of her lips betrayed a hint of the nervousness she felt.

On entering the house, Camilla found herself in a well proportioned hall, softly carpeted in a deep, glowing shade of pink. Corridors flanked a wide, central staircase, and here, too, were the inevitable roses, arranged artistically in crystal bowls on small tables, filling the air with their perfume, so that Camilla was convinced that as long as she lived the scent of roses would remind her of her first arrival at Ratnagalla.

All the doors leading off the corridors were closed, and the house had an unnaturally silent feel.

'Mother?' Phillip called impatiently. 'We're home. Where are you?'

The door to their immediate left opened soundlessly, and a young woman tiptoed out, closing it behind her with infinite care not to make a noise. She was slim almost to the point of being thin, and this was emphasised by her close fitting day dress with long, tight sleeves, in a shade of brown which did nothing to lift her already sallow complexion. Her hair, nearly black, was caught at the nape of her neck and held in place by a net, and her finest feature, redeeming a face rather too severe, were her eyes, which were huge and velvet dark.

'Hush!' she said, a finger to her lips. 'Mother has one of her headaches.'

Phillip made a *moue* of distaste.

'Oh, hell! Today of all days!' he exclaimed. 'Oh well, I suppose it can't be helped. You'll have to look after

Cam—er, Miss Marsh, instead. My sister, Helen—Miss
Camilla Marsh.'

Helen Ballantyne looked gravely at Camilla, taking in
the petal fairness of her skin, the slender curves of her
figure and her elegantly-tailored grey riding habit, relieved only by touches of lilac which her half-mourning
permitted. In the other girl's eyes, Camilla read resentment and a trace of envy, and on her own part, she was
conscious of a desire to be sympathetic. From the set of
her mouth and her general demeanour it was obvious
that Helen was dissatisfied with life, and Camilla, alone
in this strange enviroment, had need of a female friend.

Impulsively, she held out her hand.

'Please call me Camilla,' she said. 'We are going to be
sisters, and I hope we can be friends, too.'

Helen took Camilla's hand in a brief, cool salutation,
but her face remained unsmiling. Most of her interest
seemed to be centred on Camilla's clothes.

'I wasn't aware that costumes had become quite so
masculine,' she observed bluntly. 'We don't see the
latest fashions from England very much, up here.'

Camilla was taken aback, but tried hard not to show it.

'When the rest of my luggage comes up, you're welcome to see what I have brought with me,' she said
evenly. 'Then your dressmaker can copy anything you
particularly like.'

'We've had a long ride, Helen,' Phillip drawled. 'I'm
sure you two will find plenty of opportunities to talk
fashion at a later date. Right now, I expect Camilla
would be glad of a chance to rest before dinner.'

His sister flashed him an angry sidelong glance.

'Right now, I should be obliged if you would lower
your voice,' she said pointedly. 'I told you—mother has
a headache.' Turning to Camilla, she said, 'Please come
with me,' and led the way upstairs.

Camilla followed Helen, and a silent and obviously
disapproving Fanny brought up the rear. The room

allotted to Camilla was small but pleasant, overlooking the garden and the long vistas of tea terraces beyond.

'I hope this will suffice for now,' Helen said, with cool politeness. 'When you are married, of course, you will occupy the master suite.'

'It's very nice. Thank you,' said Camilla. 'I do hope your mother will soon feel better.'

The other girl hesitated in the doorway, as if she had in mind to say something, then decided against it. 'Mother suffers quite a lot from headaches,' she said briefly, and added, 'Dinner is at seven, when Javier will be in from the estate. Perhaps you would like to join us in the drawing room, shortly before.'

When they were alone, Fanny helped Camilla out of her riding habit, and the girl stretched out thankfully on the bed, closing her eyes. But she was not at peace. Behind the closed lids, her mind was a turmoil of racing impressions and feverish anticipation. The long journey up through the breathtaking mountain country, the brilliant green of the tea bushes, the dark-eyed children in the village, and finally, this house in its glorious setting, drowning in roses, all jostled for place on the moving screen of her memory.

Fanny began to unpack.

'It will be a good job when the rest of your luggage is brought up from Nuwara Eliya, Miss,' she said practically. 'You've hardly a thing to wear. What shall you put on for dinner?'

Camilla opened her eyes. It should be a momentous decision, a choice of dress in which to meet her future husband, but as Fanny said, most of her luggage had not yet arrived, and partial mourning precluded a fair choice of colours.

'The pearl grey, I think,' she said. 'I always feel well in it, at least.'

Fanny nodded her approval, and then had the sense to remain silent whilst Camilla tried to rest. But it was beyond her to snatch even a few minutes sleep, for surely, soon, she would see Javier, surely nothing could further postpone their meeting. He had not been at the docks to welcome her, nor was he in the house to greet her on her arrival, and she would have been less than human had she not confessed to a sneaking disappointment. But now the time was approaching fast when he and she would come face to face, and she could scarcely contain her excitement, for this was the culmination of a lifelong dream.

Well before six-thirty, Camilla was already attired in the grey dress, slim and straight in the bodice, with all the fullness of the skirt at the back. Mechlin lace trimmed the square cut décolletage and the elbow-length sleeves. Fanny had brushed her silvery blonde hair back from the sides into a chignon, and curled it into a slight fringe over her forehead. Pearl-studded pins held her hair in place, and around her neck, the da Silva pearls gleamed softly.

She surveyed herself critically in the long cheval mirror.

'Will I do, Fanny?'

'You look just lovely, Miss Camilla. Too good for a man who can't take the time to come and welcome you properly. If you ask me, there's something strange about this family altogether, something I can't quite put my finger on . . .'

'Now, Fanny—' Camilla began warningly, but the older woman was looking out of the window, and suddenly exclaimed,

'Bless me, but this must be him!'

Camilla flew over to join her, and half-concealed by the curtain, tried to look out and remain hidden at the same time. A man was striding up the path through the garden, with long strides, taking the steps two or three at a time. From the riding boots and somewhat worn tweedy jacket it was obvious he had come straight from the estate, and in one hand he carried a battered old hat which had seen much service. But in spite of his none too elegant attire, he had an unmistakable air of authority, a proud and aristocratic bearing. There was a kind of hauteur in his face, which was unsmiling, and creased with lines of tiredness. He was clean-shaven, and his hair was a rich, dark brown with the sheen of chestnut here and there as the sun caught it—the infamous red streak of the Ballantynes. This, without doubt, was Javier da Silva Ballantyne.

'My word—a fine figure of a man!' Fanny murmured involuntarily. 'I shouldn't like to get on the wrong side of him, though!'

The man checked his stride as he came to the verandah, paused and stood for a moment, looking thoughtfully out over the garden, and running a hand wearily through the sleek, shining hair. Then he turned to go inside, and in that instant, glanced upward. Camilla, in her eagerness, had stepped out from behind the curtain, and found herself looking directly down into his eyes. She stood transfixed, not daring to move, quite sure that he had seen her, for a faint, derisive smile curled his lips. Then he looked away, dismissively, and walked swiftly into the house.

CHAPTER
TWO

CAMILLA'S heart thudded so hard she could hear its
pounding in her ears and she felt as if she were being
slowly suffocated. Forcing herself to remain still, she
took several deep breaths to regain her composure, but
she knew that something irrevocable had happened to
her in that short interval when her eyes met those of the
man below. His smile could hardly be called welcoming,
in fact it seemed to say that he could not care less if she
were here or not. But here she was, and something in
him had struck an answering chord deep in her own
nature. On some barely understood, subconscious level,
she recognised him, and she was going to make him
admit that recognition, acknowledge that he could not
so easily disregard her. She patted her already impecc-
able hairstyle into place, took one last look at herself in
the mirror and announced, 'I think I shall go down now,
Fanny.'

'It's early, Miss,' Fanny demurred.

'Miss Ballantyne said "shortly before seven" did she
not? It's a question of how one interprets "shortly". Oh,
Fanny, don't you think I have waited long enough to
meet him?'

There was no gainsaying Camilla once she had made
up her mind, and she was out of the room and half way
along the corridor before the maid had shrugged her
shoulders in resignation to the inevitable.

She located the drawing-room easily, because the
door was slightly ajar, and the voices of the occupants
drifted up to her as she came down the stairs.

'Really, Javier, I do think you might have gone straight up to change for dinner, today at least.'

A voice Camilla had not heard before, husky and very faintly accented, with a slight, febrile undertone of excitability.

'I don't see why, mother. Every evening at this time, I come in from the fields and have a whisky and soda, which I consider I've more than earned, since my day begins at six a.m. I fail to understand why I should alter my routine, which is going to remain essentially unchanged whether I am married or single.'

Camilla caught her breath and stopped dead in her tracks, one hand on the polished wooden banister rail. It was the voice which first arrested her, rich, deep, calm, slightly sardonic, it matched so perfectly the man she had seen enter the house so short a time before. The practical, somewhat cynical nature of his words came as a secondary shock. She supposed vaguely that she should have proceeded on her way to the drawing-room and let her entrance put a stop to the conversation there and then, but she could not move, it was as if her whole body were paralysed.

'I know—indeed, who should know better—that a planter's wife must accommodate herself to the routine of the estate,' the woman's voice replied. 'But the girl has only arrived today. I have not even met her myself, and I do feel you owe her the courtesy of a proper welcome.'

Camilla felt her cheeks redden; 'the girl' could only be herself. The woman's voice had taken on a nervous, rising edge, and her son said, with a gentleness that Camilla had not expected, 'Mother, don't worry. I know how to conduct myself, and you need have no fear I shall forget my manners. There—now I have finished my drink, I shall go upstairs and return shortly, a model of sartorial elegance.'

There was no way Camilla could have avoided a

precipitate meeting, nor could she appear not to have heard what she did. The door of the drawing-room opened fully, and there she was, almost at the bottom of the stairs. He was so tall that standing in the hall below her his eyes were level with hers, and she saw that they were the tawny colour of old port, flecked with gold. The dark-etched eyebrows rose, and he looked her over, his expression forbidding.

Old platitudes about attack being the best method of defence, and taking the bull by the horns, sprang to Camilla's mind, so she plunged boldly ahead, even though his gaze reduced her to the status of a recalcitrant schoolgirl.

'I could not help overhearing what you said,' she observed, keeping her voice cool and her smile unabashed. 'I do hope you will not feel obliged to change your routine in any way on my account. I shall be happy to fit in with the household in every way.'

His unwavering regard continued for a moment longer. Quietly, he said, 'Then we shall understand each other very well. Will you excuse me?' And went swiftly past her, up the stairs.

It had hardly been the romantic meeting Camilla's youthful imagination had been conjuring up for so many years. As meetings go, it could not have been less fortuitous. However much she would have liked to believe it, Camilla could not deceive herself that this man had been yearning anxiously and eagerly for the arrival of his prospective bride. He was busy, indifferent, and had only just managed to keep the promise of courtesy he had made to his mother.

'Do come into the drawing-room. You are, perhaps, a little early, but it will give us time to get acquainted.'

Doña Lucia was in command of herself again, and did not hesitate to put the blame for her son's manner squarely on Camilla's shoulders. She should not have come down to dinner before she was expected, and then she would not have encountered Javier before he was suitably attired, rested, and ready to meet her, her words insinuated.

Doña Lucia Ballantyne da Silva had undoubtedly been a good-looking woman in her youth, and was still handsome now. She had the same proud, erect carriage that Javier had, and where Helen's skin tended to sallowness, her mother's was olive, and complimented perfectly the expressive dark eyes and raven black hair, with only a few traces of grey. She wore black, as Camilla was to discover she always did, and there was something in the quick, emotional gestures of her hands, the constant flickering of her eyes, which suggested a highly nervous temperament.

The two women sat side by side and talked generalities. Camilla inquired politely if Doña Lucia's headache was better, and was told that it was, but she suffered frequently from them, and on those occasions the house had to be kept very quiet. Camilla did not think that she and Fanny would be the cause of any great disturbance, but promised dutifully to bear this in mind, and tacked away on the subject of her admiration of the garden, and particularly the roses. At this, Doña Lucia's face came alive with enthusiasm, and she launched herself into a lecture on rose-growing and the many different varieties, whilst Camilla sat and listened, glad to have said the right thing.

They were interrupted by the arrival of Phillip, changed for dinner and looking very smart and the image of a portrait hanging over the fireplace which, Camilla decided, must have been Edgar Ballantyne as a young man.

'Ah, Felipe,' said his mother, and the younger Ballantyne winced visibly. Only the eldest of her children had been given a Portuguese name, but it made no difference to Doña Lucia, the other two were always 'Felipe' and 'Elena' to her.

Helen made her appearance soon after, in an emerald green dress which suited her colouring much better than the brown she had worn earlier. Camilla noted that both she and her mother still wore the bustle, which was fading out of fashion in England, and recalled her grandmother saying that by the time the latest styles filtered through to the outposts of Empire, they were already *demodé* in the land of their origination.

The drawing-room windows were open onto the verandah, and when Javier, soberly dark suited and immaculate, completed the gathering, he turned to Camilla and said with faultless courtesy, 'Would you care to come out onto the verandah and watch our sunset?'

Surprised, she said, 'Thank you, I should like that very much.' And almost as if he had never subjected her to that withering stare not so very long before, he escorted her out and saw she was seated comfortably on one of the cane chairs.

A servant brought out a trolley of drinks, and Javier stretched out his long frame on the chair opposite hers, a glass of whisky in one hand.

'The moment of the day every planter is supposed to relish most—at least, in the familiar stereotype we present,' he said, with a touch of self-mockery.

'And do they? Do you?' Camilla could not resist asking. He had not asked her about her journey, enquired after her health or her family, or any of the normal subjects discussed by two people meeting for the first time, but had launched into conversation as if they had known each other for many years, and could safely dispense with formalities. She was intrigued by this unconventional approach, but could not help wondering if it were expressly intended to throw her off balance.

Javier was looking directly at her.

'I don't know. It has much to recommend it, but so has the moment when one first rides out in the early morning, when everything is so still and fresh, and the hills themselves are only half awake.'

They were scarcely out of earshot of the little group in the drawing-room. Camilla could hear the murmur of their conversation, and Phillip's occasional loud laughter. But for all that they might have been alone, he and she, alone with the splendour of the swiftly dying sun, the crimson sky and the now silent hills, the long shadows encroaching the garden so that the roses stood breathless, sculptured like alabaster. And Camilla knew already where this man's abiding passion lay, or he could not have spoken so poetically of the land that belonged to him. A woman who set herself up as a rival to Ratnagalla would lose him—no, she would never approach him nearly enough to inspire his affection or his respect. She must become an ally, must find herself a place in the scheme of things, so that she, too, would belong. To Camilla, already half in love with the country, and fascinated by the man, it seemed straightforward enough. She was to recall the naïve and simple faith of that first evening many times, ruefully, in the months to come.

The dinner that evening was a culinary triumph as fine as any Camilla had tasted in the dining rooms of English stately homes, but the Ballantynes did not appear to consider it anything exceptional. Apparently they were accustomed to this standard of cuisine, and took it for granted.

'Yes, we have a very fine cook-factotum who came out here with my late husband from Assam,' Doña Lucia said airily, in response to Camilla's praise of the food. 'Quite a number of people would love to poach him from us, I'm sure, but how we should ever replace him if he left, I really cannot imagine.'

'Lal will never leave Ratnagalla,' Javier said confidently. 'He has been here too long, and regards the place as much his as ours. Besides, he feels he owes us a debt of honour because of the trouble father took for Mohini.'

'I should think so, too!' Helen said explosively. 'An expensive mission school education for a native girl!'

Javier ignored this interruption and explained politely to Camilla.

'Mohini is Lal's only daughter, and he was made a widower when the girl was very young. Father paid for her to be educated at a mission school in Colombo. She returned to Ratnagalla not long ago, and works here as a maid. She's an intelligent girl, and it seems a waste, but there's not a great deal an educated girl of her sort can do.'

Camilla said, 'I see,' but Helen seemed to find this subject annoying in the extreme, and would not relinquish it so easily.

'She could be married and have a string of children like the Tamil women do, if she didn't think herself a cut above the field hands. All that money spent so that she could learn to read and write and give herself airs and graces!'

Javier said patiently, 'She would have considered herself above the field hands, education or no, because she and Lal are Bengalis, and he has always looked down on the Tamils and taught her to do the same, as you very well know.' Aside, to Camilla, he said, 'Lal is a tower of strength, and as my mother says, he's irreplaceable, but he's always had this thing about the indentured Tamil labourers, whom he doesn't consider in any way his equal—in which, one has to admit, he does not differ from the native Sinhalese, who feel much the same.'

'There is friction, then, between the two peoples?' Camilla asked interestedly, and was rewarded by a mild, if guarded appreciation of her interest in Javier's gold-flecked eyes.

'There is some, of course, and might be more if it were not for the fact that their lives are virtually separate. The Tamil labourers and their families live, work and exist almost entirely on the estate. The Sinhalese resent their presence, but since they won't work for us we are obliged to find an alternative. They speak different languages—Sinhala is Sanskrit-based and akin to the languages of northern India, and Tamil is a southern, Dravidian tongue. Furthermore, the Sinhalese are Buddhists and the Tamils are Hindus.'

Phillip clapped his hands.

'Bravo, Javier! An excellent and learned resume of our native problems!' he applauded, grinning.

His brother's smile held no rancour, but no approval either. Undisturbed, he said, 'If Camilla is to live here, these are facts she needs to know. There are some of us who like to get to the bottom of things, rather than merely to coast along the surface.'

'As for me, I make a damn good coaster,' Phillip said jauntily.

'Felipe!' his mother reprimanded sharply, and he had sufficient wit to scowl down at his plate, rather than at her.

'I still think,' Helen said to Camilla, in a low voice so that no one else heard her, 'that it is criminal to spend so much on that girl's education, whereas I have not even been to Europe, yet.'

Camilla said evenly, 'There is nothing in Europe so beautiful as what you have here, believe me, Helen.'

'I'm not interested in scenery, I'm interested in finding myself a husband,' the other girl muttered. 'Although, maybe they are not so plentiful, since *you* had to come here to find one.'

The sheer, intentional malice of this remark took Camilla's breath away. She glanced quickly around the table to see if anyone else had heard, but they did not. Helen had picked her moment and made sure there was sufficient conversation to allow her low utterance to pass unnoticed.

Camilla was not going to argue on this level. She had

come prepared to offer friendship, but up to now her forays in that direction had been rebuffed or ignored. She followed her grandmother's dictum of treating the contemptible and unpleasant as if it did not exist, and although she was stung, tried hard not to show it.

All in all, she was glad to retire to her room at the end of a long and tiring day, crowded with experiences, to submit herself to the soothing ministrations of Fanny, and to fall between the sheets and almost immediately blot out the world in sleep.

She was woken in the morning by a gentle tapping on her door, and at first could not remember where she was. Blinking, she sat up and called, 'Come in,' fully expecting it to be Fanny.

But it was not. The girl who brought in her tray of early morning tea wore a plain, dark blue, white-collared dress of the type any servant-girl might wear. A European dress on an Indian girl, slim and graceful as a wand, her black hair pinned neatly back under a prim, starched cap, the severity of which only accentuated the gentle beauty of her face, the sweetly curved mouth and enormous eyes, fringed by the longest lashes Camilla had ever seen.

'I've brought your tea, Miss,' she said, and her voice was soft and cultured.

Camilla smiled in return. She felt an immediate kinship with this girl, she could not have said why.

'You must be Mohini—Lal's daughter,' she said.

'That's right, Miss.'

'Javier—Mr Ballantyne—told me about you. You went to a mission school in Colombo, didn't you?'

'Yes, Miss. That was where I became accustomed to dressing this way.' She gestured expressively at her skirts. 'I cannot wear a sari now, I feel strange—foreign. It isn't an affectation.'

She stopped sharply, as if afraid she was talking too much, but the new young memsahib was smiling at her in a friendly and quite uncondescending manner.

'I'm sure it isn't. It's simply what one is used to, I suppose,' Camilla agreed. 'Did you like the school?'

'Oh, yes!' Mohini was enthusiastic. 'I learned so much, there. I love to read, whenever I have the time. And I am a Christian, too,' she added proudly, 'although of this my father does not approve.'

No, Camilla thought, he would not. But presumably, he had wanted his daughter to have an education, and at mission schools, religion went hand in hand with reading and writing.

Mohini set the tray on Camilla's knees, and draped a thin wrap around her shoulders.

'I must go. There is work to do in the kitchen,' she said, and it was just possible to discern from her polite young voice that she found that work distasteful.

Camilla sipped her tea, and wondered thoughtfully if Edgar Ballantyne had fully realised the consequences of sending his old servant's daughter to be educated in Colombo. True, the girl had charm, beauty and intelligence, but what was her future, alienated from her own culture, and unacceptable in the one she had so thoroughly adopted? It came to Camilla as a sudden shock that as the prospective mistress of Ratnagalla she would most likely be the one upon whom this problem devolved. There and then, she decided that the girl should be her especial concern.

After she had drunk her tea Camilla could no longer resist the fresh and fragrant morning she could see outside her window. She decided she must get up. Merely from gazing out at the gardens, still glistening with dew, and the hills, standing out clear and sharp against the sky, as if newly-washed by the mists that had just lifted from their highest peaks, she understood Javier's reference to the loveliness of the mornings at Ratnagalla.

She was downstairs, dressed for the day and ready for

whatever it might bring, not long after six-thirty, to the astonishment of the Tamil servant she met in the hall, bearing away the remains of the master's breakfast. From him, she elucidated that neither the mistress nor the young mistress left their rooms much before ten-thirty, and that the *Periya Durai* was on the verandah, if he had not already left.

Pleased with herself for being able to pick up so readily the Tamil she had not used since her childhood in Madras, Camilla made her way to the verandah, where she found the 'big master' just about to set out for the fields. He was wearing the same old jacket as when she had first met him yesterday, trousers tucked into leather boots, and the battered hat lay on one of the cane tables. His eyebrows rose in faint surprise at the sight of her.

'Good Lord! Are you habitually such an early riser?' he demanded. 'I'm usually the only person alive at this hour, apart from the servants.'

'It was such a lovely morning, I couldn't bear to lie in bed any longer,' she replied serenely.

'Yes. Well, my mother will not be up for some time. If she has a migraine you will not see her before luncheon. Helen usually stays in her room reading romantic novels or some such nonsense. Phillip is not enamoured of the early mornings, either, unless he has a whim to go for a ride, in which case, you might like to accompany him.'

'I would prefer to accompany you,' she said impulsively.

'That's not possible,' he said curtly. 'I am always in the fields before seven, after which I am either in the factory or the office. As it is, I seldom seem to get through the amount of work there is, and I certainly can't spare the time to take ladies on pleasure jaunts.'

Camilla bit her lip. She had not intended him to take time off from the work of the estate to amuse her. What she meant was, she wanted to go with him on his rounds, to see what the life and work of a tea estate entailed. But he did not give her time to rephrase her request.

'I must go,' he said, picking up his hat. 'I may see you at luncheon—otherwise, we shall meet for dinner. Good day.'

He was off down the path with his long, impatient stride before Camilla had chance to say a word, leaving her to muse on the sad fact that where he was concerned, she had scarcely put a foot right since her arrival. But how could she, if he would insist on misconstruing her words and her actions, if he refused to spare her even a little of his precious time so that they could get to know one another?

Camilla sighed, and sat down in one of the cane chairs. A servant came to ascertain what she would like for breakfast, and she asked simply for tea, toast and pre-serves.

Already, the quiet of the morning was being pervaded by the noises of a busy, working estate, the shouts of the pluckers as they moved along the tea terraces, the faint clanking and humming of machinery from the factory. These hills would be alive with activity throughout the day, until the tea was brought down in baskets carried on the heads of the pluckers, to be weighed and sorted. Even then, when night fell and the hills were quiet, at busy times the work in the factory might continue through the night, a ceaseless round of withering, roll-ing, drying and fermenting, to achieve the finished product, the fine, black leaf which made the fragrant, increasingly popular drink.

After breakfast, Camilla went for a brief ride with Phillip, as Javier had indicated she might, and his brother seemed keen for her company. It seemed that what he said about taking no interest in the estate and playing no part in its management was entirely true; where Ratnagalla was concerned, Phillip Ballantyne was a passenger only. He lost no time in confiding to Camil-la, whilst out on their ride, that he hated everything to do with tea planting, and wished only that Javier would sell up so that they could all go to live in England.

'Is there any likelihood of his doing so?' Camilla asked.

'Not a ghost of a chance, my dear Camilla. He thinks the sun rises and sets only over Ratnagalla. Javier will never willingly leave Ceylon. Unfortunately, the only place I've ever felt at home was in England, where I was at school. I'd like to be an English country squire, with a nice house somewhere in the shires, a moderate income, and leisure to lead a civilised existence.'

Phillip dug his heels angrily into his horse's flank, and Camilla had to spur her mount on to keep up with him. When they slowed down again, he said sullenly, 'Is it my fault I'm a younger son, whose father and brother were both so intransigently devoted to this benighted place?'

Camilla, who thought this 'benighted place' just about the most beautiful spot she had ever visited, said thoughtfully, 'But you are free to go, Phillip. Javier is not preventing you.'

'Oh, no?' There was heavy irony in the young man's voice. 'He has control of the Ballantyne money, and says the world is my oyster, but I must go out and make my own way in it. As I'm sure you have noticed, I have a natural aversion to hard work.' He laughed, but without amusement. 'My mother won't give me any money, either, although the da Silvas were loaded with it, which is no doubt the reason my father married her. What I need, Camilla, is a nice heiress, like yourself. I say, you wouldn't fancy marrying me instead of Javier, would you?'

It was said lightly, but his eyes raked her up and down in a way that was not very brotherly, and Camilla suddenly had the cold, unpleasant sensation that she had walked into a pit of dangerous animals who were not tamed, who were out for her blood, and might devour her at any time. It was essential that she put this importunate young man in his place as soon as possible, for he was not so harmless as his casually bantering manner and cultivated foppishness might suggest.

'Don't be silly, Phillip,' she said sharply. 'I think it's time we rode back to the house, or we shall be late for luncheon.'

Javier did not put in an appearance at lunch time, and Camilla learned that if he were busy, which he usually was, he had something brought down to the office so he could eat whilst dealing with the paperwork. But Doña Lucia had surfaced, and after the meal, invited Camilla to join her in the drawing-room for coffee. Helen, who thought this *tête à tête* included her also, was annoyed to find herself dismissed.

'I think we should talk about the wedding, my dear,' she said, allowing Camilla to take over the ritual of the coffee. 'You have come to Ceylon to be married, and now you are here, I feel there is no point in waiting too long.'

Camilla kept her hand steady on the coffee pot. She had arrived at Ratnagalla only the previous day, and this strange woman who was to be her mother-in-law was talking of waiting too long!

'Of course not,' she agreed diplomatically. 'But do you not think Javier and I should have, perhaps, a little time to get to know one another?'

'Time? How much time do you need—and what is it you wish to know?' Doña Lucia demanded agitatedly, her cup rattling in its saucer so that Camilla feared she would scald herself with the contents. 'You have been virtually betrothed to my son since birth, it is not as if the idea is new to you.'

Camilla waited until the older woman had put the cup down on the small table, and the fluttering of her hands had ceased.

'No, Doña Lucia, it is not, and I have thought of myself as Javier's bride for many years. But *he* is new to me, and I to him,' she pointed out, gently.

'My son is ready to marry you immediately,' Doña Lucia said emphatically, 'and believe me, he is not a man who is short of prospective brides. There are many mamas on this island who would consider him an enviable catch for their daughters, who themselves would not be averse.'

Camilla wondered if this could be taken as a threat. Marry Javier now, or there are others waiting in line. Her chin went up, and she said coolly, 'I am sure of it, ma'am. And I myself am not considered to be entirely ineligible.'

Doña Lucia's proud features quivered and seemed about to decompose before Camilla's eyes, so that she felt a stab of remorse on account of her swift and instinctive riposte.

'Please—let me pour you some more coffee,' she urged comfortingly. 'I am sure that we both desire the same thing, it is only over the details we differ slightly. As you say, I have come to Ceylon to be married.'

Doña Lucia composed herself, with a visible effort.

'I am getting a headache,' she said plaintively. Her large, dark eyes gazed reproachfully at Camilla, and she said, 'You will not "get to know" my son, as you put it, until you are married to him. He is too busy for a formal courtship, and during the day you will seldom see him. You know, in the Portuguese community it is quite common for a girl to be married to a man she scarcely knows, and, I believe, all over the Indian subcontinent the indigents have the same custom. Courtship comes after marriage. A husband and wife must perforce live closely, and share their lives. You have no mother, but I am sure your grandmother has spoken to you about marriage, so you will understand what I am saying. Marry Javier, Camilla—marry him quickly. It is the only answer.'

She leaned back in her chair, as if exhausted by so long a speech, and half closed her eyes.

Camilla considered what she had said in silence, and came to the unavoidable conclusion that there was a certain amount of truth in it. If today was to be taken as typical, and there was no reason to suppose otherwise, she would indeed see little of Javier, their acquaintance would be limited to a formal and very public hour at the dinner table. He had made it abundantly clear that he did not intend modifying his routine one whit on account of her presence, the responsibilities of the estate took priority at all times, and would continue to do so.

Here was the point where a girl with less determination, with less of the pioneering spirit in her blood and in her character, would have begun to wonder whether she could stomach marriage to such a man, who could ignore her arrival, treat her with aloof disdain, and let her know in no uncertain terms that she came a poor second to his beloved Ratnagalla.

But Camilla, although she could not deny that she had qualms, was made of stronger stuff than her slim body and fragile appearance implied. For most of her life she had believed she was destined to marry this man, and she was not going to turn tail so easily.

And there was something else. In spite of his indifference, his coolness, and his mocking attitude, there was a feeling deep within her that Javier was right for her, and she for him. Meeting him had confirmed her innermost conviction that this was the man she wanted, and in his very coldness there was an attraction, a challenge that was near irresistible. When they were married, she thought, he would not be able to avoid her, would not be able to pretend that her presence did not concern him.

An erratic little pulse began to beat in the hollow of her throat, and she put a hand there to steady it. Doña Lucia had been right about one thing—when they were man and wife, they must live in close proximity. They would—and Camilla felt the blood rising to her face and neck—they would share the same bedroom. Camilla knew, without vanity, that she was beautiful, and Javier da Silva Ballantyne was after all a man, like the others she had danced with at so many balls in England, who had whispered nonsense in her ear, and endeavoured to hold her more tightly than propriety demanded. Yes, she would marry him, and dissolve that arrogance in the warmth of the response she was more than ready to give him.

Camilla smiled at Doña Lucia, and conceded gracefully.

'Of course I will marry him, as soon as you think fit. I leave the arrangements entirely in your hands,' she said. And now, truly, she felt committed beyond the point of no return.

That evening, as they were about to go in to dinner, Javier said to Camilla, 'It occurs to me that I may have misinterpreted your request to accompany me this morning. Am I right?'

'Indeed, I believe you did,' she said, levelly and without reproach. 'Maybe I did not phrase my request properly. What I really wanted was not to distract you from your duties, but to accompany you whilst you performed them, to see a little of how the estate works.'

'You are really interested in all that?' he said doubtfully. 'It is hot out in the fields, and noisy in the factory.'

'Naturally, I am interested,' she replied. 'It is part of your life, and now part of mine. Is it strange that I should wish to know a little of what it involves?'

'It is very strange, in my experience, for a woman to want any part of the hard graft of estate life, or even to evince any interest in it,' he said. 'But if you would like to see round the estate, I will take you. Be up early tomorrow morning, and do not dress for fashion. You will need a wide-brimmed hat and a stout pair of riding boots.'

He turned away from her, closing the discussion as perfunctorily as he had begun it, but Camilla was conscious of a swift excitement, and beneath that, a deeper, more substantial satisfaction. Perhaps Javier was beginning to take her seriously as a future wife, not just an empty-headed girl out from England, who peered round curtains, and eavesdropped on private conversations.

CHAPTER
THREE

SHE was up early as he had instructed, dressed and down for breakfast on the verandah by six o'clock, in a state of eager but well-subdued expectancy. Now at last she would see something of how Ratnagalla worked, and, no less important, of the man who ran it.

Javier eyed Camilla's plain brown riding habit and sturdy boots with approval as they walked together through the gardens, still fresh with dew, to where a groom waited with two horses ready saddled.

And only now did Camilla really grasp the extent of the Ballantyne estate, as they rode over hill and valley, acre upon acre of terraced hillside rolling before them in neatly ordered fertility. The pluckers were already in the fields, men, women and older children, each group working with swift dexterity under the supervision of a *kangany*, a well-trained native foreman. Javier dismounted frequently to observe and to converse with the *kanganies* in swift, fluent Tamil, and indicated to Camilla that she should dismount, to get a closer look at how the pluckers worked.

'It's not so simple as it might appear, considering the speed at which they work,' he told her. 'It requires skill, practice and careful supervision. See how they take just the tip of the shoot, two leaves and terminal bud, between the thumb and one finger? That's called a fine pluck, and it's the way I always insist it is done at Ratnagalla.'

Camilla watched closely, noting the size of the cane baskets the pluckers carried strapped to their backs.

'They hold from fifteen to eighteen pounds of green leaf,' Javier said, following her gaze. 'It's hot, hard, heavy work, no doubt about it. But most of these labourers have escaped from a life of grinding poverty and hopelessness in Southern India to come here, so they work hard and don't complain. Later, I'll show you the lines where they live.'

Camilla began to appreciate the need for the boots as she followed Javier along steep terraces where it was difficult to stand upright, let alone work. He did not slacken his pace to accommodate her, almost as if he were saying, 'You wanted to come. This is how it is, and it's no place for a gently nurtured European woman, who has never done a day's work in her life.' But she kept up with him as well as she could, gritting her teeth with determination, and according a growing respect to the pluckers, who worked as swiftly here as they did on the lower slopes.

Eventually, he condescended to slow down, and held out his hand to help over a particularly steep patch. She did not refuse it, and in his eyes, she was gratified to see a reluctant esteem.

'You have a certain spirit, Camilla,' he admitted, 'but then, I should have expected that from the grand-daughter of Colonel Sumter. My father spoke of him always as a man of courage and integrity. I wish I had met him.'

She bit back a sudden sense of loss which threatened to bring tears to her eyes.

'It's strange how our families have remained close, without any real contact, all these years,' she remarked.

'The kind of friendship that existed between my father and your grandfather did not depend solely on geographical proximity,' he said. 'There are ties that are stronger than we know.'

'What was your father like, Javier?' she asked. 'I, too, regret not having known him.'

Javier thought for a moment, taking in the ordered activity of the scene before him.

'My father? He was an adventurer and a visionary. Mentally and physically, he was always pushing back frontiers. He always believed that the future of Ceylon was tea, and, until the day he died, he was arguing against those who said it wouldn't work—and there are still plenty who say that, in spite of what you see here. Tea is in its infancy, but I'm convinced, as he was, that it will take hold of this island's economy and make it prosper. My father loved Ceylon, loved Ratnagalla, but there was always a restlessness about him. If there had been nothing to fight for, no one to oppose him, he would have run out of steam long before he did.'

Camilla said, 'We never knew, my grandmother and I, how he died, although we think it was the shock of hearing the news which killed my grandfather.'

Javier's eyes darkened.

'I can't enlighten you. He was as strong as an ox and had never been ill. One morning we just found him dead, and not even the doctor could offer any viable explanation. However, you have lived in India and should know that sudden, unexplained deaths are not unusual. I would advise you not to speak of it at home. It upsets my mother considerably.'

'I should not dream of venturing on such a subject with your mother, unless she brought it up first,' Camilla cried indignantly, stung that he could think her capable of such tactlessness.

'No, I daresay you would not,' he responded equably, 'but I felt it my duty to warn you. My mother becomes agitated very easily, as I am sure you have noticed.' Swiftly, he changed the subject. 'Shall we go and see the factory? I've had some new machinery installed, with which my engineer is having something of a battle.'

If the size of the Ratnagalla estate had been a surprise to Camilla, the tea factory itself gave her equal food for thought. She had expected a much smaller building than this airy, spacious and obviously quite new two-storey edifice.

'This is my pride and joy,' Javier said, with unconcealed satisfaction. 'We built it only a couple of years ago, after demolishing the earlier building completely. It was useless, having been constructed as a coffee store, because tea needs so much more undercover space. Come inside—but keep well clear of the machinery.'

Fascinated, Camilla followed Javier on a brisk tour of the factory. She glanced into the dark, humid fermentation room, where the chemical changes in the leaf took place at a damp, constant temperature of 70°F. She saw men sorting leaf into various grades, from broken orange pekoe to dust and fannings, with the aid of circular bamboo mesh trays. In the drying room, leaf was being fired in machines similar to chests of drawers, one above another, heated by charcoal fires below. Upstairs, in the withering loft, the tea was spread on tiers of bamboo trays, exposed to light and air. Javier, who had given Camilla a simplified but thorough commentary on all these various processes, told her that natural withering was preferred in fine weather, but they had the use of revolving fans to circulate hot air from charcoal stoves when necessary.

'And now we had better go down again, and see how our patent revolving roller is progressing,' he said, with a wry grimace.

Around a fearsome contraption of tables, cylinders and noisily moving parts, a small, wiry, middle-aged man, grimy and oil-smeared, was endeavouring to climb in, climb out, caressing a cylinder here, adjusting a nut there, and generally attempting to get on more intimate terms with the machinery than seemed safe or reasonable to Camilla.

'Yer silly old besom!' he shouted at the offending machine, in affectionate exasperation. 'What's up wi' thee this morning, then?'

'Come out of there, Mac!' Javier raised his voice against the general din. 'I'd like you to meet Miss Marsh.'

The engineer emerged from his love/hate affair with the rolling machine, and brought it to a stop. He held out a grimy hand, then thought better of it, and instead offered Camilla a smile of such genuine welcome and delight that it warmed her heart.

'How d'ye do, Miss Marsh,' he said, in his broad, thick, north of England accent. 'It's a rare treat to see a young lady down 'ere at the factory.'

'Then I must persuade Mr Ballantyne to bring me here more often,' Camilla said brightly, including both Javier and the engineer in her smile.

'Miss Marsh wanted to see how we process the leaf,' said Javier. 'Now she has done so, I hardly think she will be a regular visitor.'

Camilla's smile faded, and she lapsed into silence as the two men began to examine the machine.

'Still not altogether happy with her, Mac? What seems to be the trouble?'

'Can't rightly say, Mr Ballantyne, but there's summat that dun't work as it should, and nowt I do seems to help. Reckon as I shall 'ave to strip 'er down and put 'er together again meself, 'afore I can understand 'er.'

'Carefully though, Mac. She's an expensive piece of equipment,' Javier frowned thoughtfully. As if suddenly remembering Camilla's existence, he said, 'Mac has been at Ratnagalla for longer than anyone cares to recall. When he first came my father mistook the accent, thought he was Scottish, whereas actually he's York-shire-born, and nicknamed him Mac.'

'There weren't nowt I could do to convince him,' the little man said cheerfully, 'so I decided I mun put up wi' it. Been Mac ever since, I 'as. Would you like some tea, Miss?'

'That would be lovely, Mac,' Camilla said gratefully, realising for the first time how hot, dishevelled and tired the round of field and factory had made her. No wonder Javier, who worked from early morning to dusk with scarcely a break, looked strained and tired in the evenings.

'Come into the office, Camilla. It's quieter and you can sit down,' said Javier.

'I'm quite all right,' the girl said defensively, but he took her arm firmly and led her through the factory to the small room full of dusty cabinets and bulging cupboards from where the business of the estate was run.

Seated on a straight, hard chair in front of Javier's over-flowing desk, thankfully sipping hot, fragrant Ratnagalla tea, she said, 'I never realised there was so much to it. Thank you for showing me.'

He laughed, and for the first time she saw a smile on his face that was not touched with mockery.

'You have only seen half,' he told her. 'There are fields we could not hope to reach in the time we have been out, some so high and so steep you'd be unable to stand. Here in Ceylon, the plucking of tea is a continuous, year-round operation, to say nothing of the pruning, planting of shade trees, looking after the young seedlings in the nursery, and so on. You'll understand why I am not a very social man.'

Camilla said, 'I don't know how you manage it all on your own.'

'Not entirely on my own. I have Mac to maintain the factory, and a number of good kanganies whom my father and I have trained. I also have an assistant, but he's on leave right now. Still, you are right, there's a lot of work to be done.'

Suddenly serious, he gazed intently and critically at her.

'You are so young, and such a slip of a girl. Do you think you can take life at Ratnagalla? It's a hardworking, isolated existence, not a round of pleasure and gaiety.'

'I can't help my youth; if it's a disadvantage, all I can say is that time will alter it,' Camilla said gravely. 'I can assure you that I'm stronger than I look. I come of generations of good, Anglo-Indian stock. And I'm not looking for a life of parties and balls.'

'What are you looking for, Camilla?' he demanded bluntly, and she stared straight back into his face, unafraid.

'Something real and vital, which I can contribute to, and be a part of,' she replied promptly.

He looked away, drained his cup, and went to a small, glazed window from where he could look out on the activities in the factory.

'Ratnagalla is real enough for anyone,' he said. 'The house, as you will have seen, runs efficiently under Lal's directions. But it needs a mistress, and my mother's health is . . .' he paused '. . . is not consistently good. She may, however, resent your encroaching on what she considers to be her territory, so you will need to be a paragon of diplomacy if you are to help without causing controversy.'

'I shall try,' Camilla promised. 'As yet, I have not met Lal. It might help if I could do so.'

'Of course. I shall see to it that you do,' he said. 'And now, if you have finished your tea, perhaps you would like a quick look at the lines before I take you back to the house.'

Events moved quickly during what remained of the day. Camilla was taken to see the kitchen, and to meet the indispensable Lal.

She had, of course, seen kitchens in Anglo-Indian households before, and was therefore not too surprised at the somewhat primitive conditions in which such delicious meals were produced. Lal's kitchen was no different—it was rudimentary, but scrupulously clean.

Lal himself was a tall, spare man well into his fifties, with ascetic features and greying hair. He had total confidence in himself, his abilities, and his place in the household, and there was nothing in the least obsequious or servile about his manner. He greeted Camilla with grave reserve, and she felt that any deference he might show her was due to his memories of her grandfather. His personal respect she would have to earn.

'I met your daughter,' she told him. 'She brings me my morning tea, as you know.'

His face brightened a little, and then clouded.

'She is a good girl,' he said. 'A little misguided, but good.'

'I found her charming, and most intelligent,' Camilla said. 'She reads a lot. This morning, we had a most interesting discussion about various books.'

Lal sniffed politely.

'Western learning,' he said. 'I should not have let her go to that place in Colombo. I wanted her only to learn to read and write, not to forsake the ways of her own people.'

'The two often go together, Lal,' Camilla pointed out.

Edgar Ballantyne's loyal old factotum looked down at Camilla with puzzled regret. Clearly, he was at a loss to understand the transformation the years in Colombo had wrought in Mohini. He had expected her to come back educated, but still a good, dutiful Hindu daughter, intact in her own culture. Instead, she had changed her religion, her outlook, her mode of dress—even her thought patterns were no longer akin to his, or so it seemed.

He said, 'I am a Hindu, memsahib. We accept within our fold only those who are born into it. To adopt an alien belief is unnecessary—truth may be found in our own path. To try to convert others to our way is, we believe, wrong. What those people in Colombo have done to my daughter will bring her no good. She no longer knows who she is. I am an old man. Who will care about her when I am gone?'

'I will, Lal,' Camilla said steadily. She did not know if he believed her, if she could convince him of the depth of interest and concern she already felt for his daughter. 'I keep my word, as my grandfather did before me,' she said, switching suddenly to a dimly-remembered Bengali she had learned long ago in Calcutta. In the sad eyes which looked into hers, a glimmer of hope showed briefly; the beginning of a mutual trust was established.

After dinner that evening Javier spent some time alone with his mother in her room, and Camilla was uncomfortably aware that her future was being discussed. She did not see Doña Lucia again, but Javier came back into the drawing-room, where Helen was playing half-heartedly on the piano, whilst Camilla occupied herself with some embroidery.

'It is a fine evening,' he said. 'Shall we take a walk in the garden?'

He addressed himself exclusively to Camilla, and her heart began to pound. The fact that he had been closeted with Doña Lucia for the past hour indicated to her that he had something of importance to discuss with her, and the invitation was not as casual as it might appear.

Outside, the night was pleasantly mild, and with a light, fringed shawl around her shoulders, Camilla was warm enough. The stars seemed to swing low and incredibly brilliant in the southern sky, and the moon lent a sharp clarity to the outline of the hills. The air was drenched with the perfume of roses, and the whole scene was unbelievably romantic, so why did she have this cold knot of apprehension in her throat? She dared not look up at Javier as he paced slowly at her side along the balustraded terrace.

I went to talk to you about our marriage,' he said, brisk but serious.

Camilla merely nodded, she was incapable of speech,

and he went on, 'As you will have gathered, I have been discussing the wedding arrangements with my mother. The date she suggests is March 12th, which is two weeks hence—if that would be agreeable to you?'

Camilla swallowed hard. They were talking about an event which would join her to this man at her side in a deep and indissoluble union, but he spoke in a cool, businesslike tone, as if he were arranging a date for transporting a cargo of tea to the docks.

'Perfectly agreeable,' she said, in a voice which matched his for calm detachment. 'I have put myself entirely at your mother's disposal with regard to the wedding arrangements.'

'Good. Then you will not object to a quiet wedding?' he said. 'To be married in church at Nuwara Eliya would involve all concerned in a considerable journey, for which my mother does not feel she has the strength. Instead, we shall ask Reverend Fielding to come to Ratnagalla and marry us here. My mother wanted the priest from Colombo, and the full rites of the Catholic church, but I persuaded her you might be happier with the Anglican vicar.'

'I certainly think my grandmother would be happier,' Camilla agreed, 'and since *she* cannot be present, a quiet wedding would suit me. I don't care to be married in front of a church full of strangers. Were you raised as a Roman Catholic, Javier?'

'Good Lord, no!' he said shortly. 'My mother has always practised her religion devoutly, but my father would have nothing to do with organised religion, of whatever denomination, so his influence more than countered hers. Being so remote precludes us from becoming ardent churchgoers, anyway.'

They strolled down the pathway between the lawns, and Camilla had the strangest sensation that the roses were suffocating her. This marriage was rushing towards her, now, with a speed she could not control, and yet

Javier had never said anything to make her believe he desired her for his wife. Was she supposed merely to infer this from the fact that things were going ahead?

He paused suddenly, looking down at her intently. Impelled to meet his gaze, she stood as still as the flowers, conscious that now he was going to tell her something deeply significant.

'What we have been discussing are mere details,' he said. 'On the other hand, what I am going to say to you now is crucial, if we are to go ahead with what is planned.

'I must be honest with you, Camilla. You are marrying me to fulfill the wishes of your grandparents, and also, I think, because you have a feeling for this part of the world and want to settle here. Am I right?'

She took a deep breath.

'Yes. I would say that's a fair definition,' she replied. It was not, she admitted to herself, wholly true, for it left out the strange sense of destiny she felt about their union, left out, also, the growing physical attraction, which made her intensely aware of him whenever he was near her. But she could hardly tell him that.

'I am marrying you for much the same family reasons,' he said, 'and also because the time is approaching when, owing to my mother's indisposition, Ratnagalla will need a mistress who is young and capable.'

She said, 'I understand.'

'Do you?' he demanded, still subjecting her to the same relentless scrutiny. 'What I am saying is that this is a marriage of convenience, Camilla, a business arrangement, if you like. I do not expect, or even desire you to demonstrate any affection for me, or to pretend to feelings which we both know are absent from the transaction, although I hope we shall respect one another and live amicably under the same roof. Is all this perfectly clear and acceptable to you?'

'Absolutely,' Camilla said calmly, and knew that she lied. Oh, if he wanted it that way, they could start out cool and business-like, but her secret and ardent hope was that once they were married and truly living together, that coolness would disperse like the mists that clung to the mountain peaks each morning, before the sun rose in its glory to chase them away.

Maybe it was wrong of her to accept a man thus, under false pretences, when he had been scrupulously honest with her. But Camilla had heard it said that all was fair in love and war, and she was campaigning for her future—and for his.

Looking down at the pathway, blanched white in the moonlight, she knew with certainty that she could not go ahead with this marriage unless she believed, deep within herself, that one day he would wake up, turn to her, and say, 'I love you, my dearest.' She would *make* him love her. It had to be, because she had already given him her heart, although he did not know it, and had expressly forbidden her to do so.

Preparations for the wedding went ahead swiftly. Camilla was now out of the official period of mourning for her grandfather, and Doña Lucia was insistent that the girl should wear the wedding dress she herself had worn, which had adorned several generations of da Silva brides.

'It needs only a little alteration,' she said excitedly. 'As a bride I was as slender as you, and only a little taller. Be careful where you are putting those pins, girl!'

This admonition was to Mohini, who, as an accomplished seamstress, had been called in from her kitchen duties, and was now crawling around on the floor, pinning up the hem.

Camilla considered her reflection in the glass. The stiffened bodice and yards of old, ivory-coloured lace made her look like something from an age long past. But it had a certain romantic appeal, it spoke of tradition and continuity, so she was glad to wear it, especially if it pleased Doña Lucia, who was becoming more emotional as the day drew nearer, as if she herself were the bride.

Mohini stood up and surveyed her handiwork.

'You look beautiful, Miss Camilla!' she declared, a wistful expression in her eyes which seemed to say that she, too, would love to be the bride wearing this European wedding-gown.

Helen's face was frankly envious as she helped fix on the old-fashioned head-dress with its band of tightly sewn seed pearls, and masses of veiling, which lent Camilla an air of mysterious sanctity, like a sacrificial virgin.

'We shall have to let it down again when it comes to my turn to wear it,' she remarked pointedly, and received a sharp look from her mother.

'That time has not come yet,' Doña Lucia said forbiddingly.

'But why not? Camilla is younger than I am,' Helen said insistently.

'Elena, at the moment I am fully occupied with your brother's wedding,' her mother said, in a tone which brooked no argument.

Camilla pushed back the veil from her face. She was tightly corseted, and was finding it difficult to breathe.

'I think you will have to let out these stays a little, Fanny, or I shall faint at the altar,' she observed.

Fanny helped her mistress out of the beautiful but constricting dress and into her everyday clothes once more with a protective air and silent disapproval written on every line of her thin face. Privately, she had already expressed to Camilla her misgivings over the entire procedure. This hole and corner wedding, as she called it, wasn't right. The grand-daughter of Colonel and Lady Sumter should be married in a proper church, in full view of a proper congregation, not tucked away in the private chapel of a practising Roman Catholic. She whispered the last words with all the distrustful fear of the Scarlet Woman of Rome which had haunted the English proletariat for the last three centuries, and evoked echoes of the fires of Smithfield.

'The Anglican vicar will officiate,' Camilla had tried to soothe her fears. 'It's simply to spare Doña Lucia the tiring journey into Nuwara Eliya. I shall not really miss having a full congregation watching me, since they would be neither family nor friends. As for the private chapel, it is simply a room Doña Lucia uses for her devotions.'

'That's as may be!' Fanny snorted. 'You'll be saying next that it would be all the same if you were led three times round the fire for your wedding, like them idolatrous Hindoos!'

Camilla could not resist a giggle.

'You sound like Mohini!' she said.

'And if I do, Miss? That's a good girl who has seen the light and given up heathen ways!' Fanny reproved.

'She's a sweet girl, I'm fond of her, and I'm sure her convictions are sincere,' Camilla said patiently. 'All I am trying to point out is, what matters is that I'm going to marry Javier. All the rest is hair-splitting.'

'I wish you wouldn't marry him, Miss Camilla,' the older woman said, with sudden fervour. 'I wish you'd call it all off, while there's still time, and go back to England. Your grandmother would understand. She wouldn't want you to be unhappy.'

There was such urgency in Fanny's voice that Camilla was arrested by it.

'Why—Fanny!' she cried. 'What makes you think I'm going to be unhappy?'

'Because that fine gentleman doesn't care for you, Miss,' the maid said sadly. 'He may be an efficient planter, and I won't deny he works hard. He may be handsome, but handsome is as handsome does, and if you love him, he'll destroy you. There—I should not have said it, but I've been with the Sumters many years, and I feel I owe it to them to say what's on my mind.'

Camilla sat quietly for a while, not answering. She had too much respect for this woman who had spent her life in Lady Sumter's service to dismiss her observations out of hand. It's true that Javier does not love me, she admitted to herself, and a little doubt crept into her mind, shaking her innate confidence that she could and *must* win his love. Because if she failed, then Fanny was right. Javier would destroy her—with his indifference.

But the alternative was to call off the wedding and return to England, to concede failure before she had even tried, and that was unthinkable. Javier was prepared to marry her, even though he insisted it was only a marriage of convenience, and it was a chance she had to take. She could not give him up. She could not leave Ratnagalla, the place towards which she felt all her life had been leading her, could not leave the man with whom she had so swiftly and completely fallen in love.

'I appreciate your intentions in speaking out as you did,' Camilla said, after a long pause. 'I know you only have my interests at heart, and much of what you said may be true. But you see, Fanny, it's too late for me to take your advice, even if I wanted to. I must, and I will marry Javier. I love him.'

Fanny's shoulders rose and fell in a slight shrug, which indicated that she had run out of arguments.

'In that case, Miss, we shall have to make the best of things,' she said practically.

Camilla jumped up and hugged her, impulsively.

'Dear Fanny! Whatever would I do without you here with me?' she exclaimed.

'That, Miss, is one problem you won't have to worry about,' Fanny said stoically. 'Your grandmother sent me with you to look after you, and that's precisely what I intend doing!'

The morning of Camilla's wedding day dawned fine and clear, like any other morning at Ratnagalla. It was hard to believe that in a matter of weeks, all this side of the island would be in the grip of the south-west monsoon, that heavy storm clouds would mass over the peaks, and torrential rain would beat down.

Camilla slept late, as brides are traditionally supposed to do. That is to say, she stayed in bed later than usual, although she was awake at first light and in the grip of a rising fever of excitement. It was hard to lie still and wait docilely for Mohini to bring her tea, and, later, her breakfast, for today she would not be allowed to join the family downstairs.

She knew that Javier had ridden out early on his rounds, as he always did. Although a minimum of work was being done on the estate today, and Ratnagalla was as close to being on holiday as it was ever likely to be, there were still essential tasks he refused to shirk. She had heard him go out, heard his brisk, unmistakable footsteps on the verandah, and his voice calling authoritatively for the groom to bring his horse.

With a small sigh she had turned over in her bed and feigned sleep, although she knew it was impossible. This time tomorrow she would wake, not here, but in the big master suite that was prepared for them, she would wake with her husband at her side, in the bed where they had spent the night together.

She stretched her arms above her head, and a shiver of anticipation coursed through her, and she wondered what it would be like to be alone with him, in the privacy of their bedroom. Closing her eyes, she imagined him taking her in his arms, kissing her . . . Beneath the high-handed and stern exterior, she sensed a passionate nature, and in herself, she knew, there was a need to respond to it. Camilla was nervous, but not afraid. Once they had made love, she was convinced the situation between them would be changed completely. She was ready—indeed, she confessed a little shamefully to her-self, she was eager for him to make love to her.

In no time at all, it seemed, Fanny was waiting to help her dress and do her hair. She had brought Mohini to help her, since it took two of them to lace Camilla into her stays and do up all the complicated hooks and fasteners, all the underpinnings of the dress.

'You'd make a good lady's maid,' Fanny said ap-provingly to the young Indian girl, whose golden skin flushed with pleasure at the compliment. 'You're quick to learn, and you understand clothes. You are wasted in the kitchen. Now, watch carefully how I do Miss Camil-la's hair.'

Mohini stood quietly, her grave dark gaze fixed on Camilla in her finery, the long lashes partly veiling her eyes. It was impossible to guess what thoughts were going through her mind. Envy, ambition, pleasure—all were hidden behind the impassive stare, and Camilla thought briefly that this girl had unsuspected depths.

'You're beautiful, Miss Camilla!' Fanny said, tears in her eyes as she stood back to take a long look at her finished handiwork. 'Oh, your grandmother would be so proud, if she could see you today. And your poor grandfather! All the years you were growing up, they longed for this day, and now it's come. You're the loveliest bride ever, I declare!'

The radiance of Camilla's smile lit up the room. She took Fanny's thin, veinous hands in her own smooth, young ones, and said, 'Thank you, Fanny, for every-thing. Be happy for me today.' Sensing the Indian girl standing silent and a little left out of this emotional tableau, she held out a hand to her. 'You too, Mohini. May we all be happy together, here at Ratnagalla.'

CHAPTER
FOUR

CAMILLA negotiated the staircase with extreme care in her long, extravagantly petticoated skirts. In the hall, Phillip, more elegant than ever, his bronzed hair brushed and gleaming, waited to offer her his arm, and Helen, whom the excitement of the day had infected so that even she was smiling a little, helped her with her train.

'And how is Ceylon's most beautiful bride this morning?' Phillip said unctuously, giving her a lazy, sidelong smile.

'Very well, thank you,' Camilla replied demurely.

'I should say so—you look quite dazzling. My brother is a lucky dog,' he said, unrepentantly irreverent.

In Doña Lucia's little chapel, the Reverend Fielding, who had arrived at Ratnagalla the night before, was ready and waiting to perform the ceremony, and Doña Lucia herself was also present, proud and stiff in her unrelieved black.

But through the layers of veiling, Camilla's eyes were fixed on the tall figure of Javier, waiting at the altar, the sunlight streaming through the small, high window picking out the chestnut glints in his dark hair. His back was firm and resolute, and only as she drew level with him did he turn his head slightly to look down at her.

For a moment, Camilla looked full into the unsmiling, gold-flecked eyes, and briefly she saw, or imagined she saw, his gaze soften a little as he took in the slim figure in the baroque splendour of the da Silva wedding finery. Then once again the proud lines of his face reasserted themselves over this momentary lapse, as the ageless words of the marriage ceremony filled the room with their solemnity. Camilla stood in a dream, repeating her vows, and listening to his resonant voice as he made his. Their hands were joined, and she felt him slip the heavy gold ring onto her finger.

'Those whom God hath joined together, let no man put asunder,' intoned the Reverend Fielding. She was Mrs Javier da Silva Ballantyne. For better or for worse.

Then it was all over. There was champagne for everyone in the drawing-room, and all the house servants filed in, smiling, to pay their respects to the new Mrs Ballantyne. Standing at Javier's side, accepting their shy congratulations, Camilla found it hard to believe, in spite of the ceremony which had so recently taken place, that she was truly married.

'Do you feel different?' Helen asked, eyeing her new sister-in-law with avid curiosity, anxious to experience vicariously what had up to now been denied her.

'I've hardly had chance to get used to it yet,' she laughed.

'Ask her tomorrow,' Phillip whispered lewdly under his breath, taking care to ensure that neither Javier not his mother was listening. If he were expecting Camilla to blush with embarrassment, he was disappointed, for she merely turned her face away contemptuously. It was Helen who reddened, a deep flush creeping up her neck beneath the sallow skin.

'Phillip, you're disgusting!' she muttered, but he was undismayed, and declaring that he had not as yet kissed the bride, took Camilla in his arms and proceeded to do so, with more thoroughness than was necessary.

'I think that will be quite sufficient,' Javier said coldly, separating them with a look that froze Camilla's blood, and made even Phillip look faintly abashed.

'When I first came to Ratnagalla, after your father and I were married,' Doña Lucia remembered suddenly, 'he insisted I put on my wedding dress and took me down the lines, so that all the field hands could see me. I asked him if it were a custom on tea estates, and he said, "I don't rightly know, but it is now".'

Javier held out a hand to Camilla.

'Then let us keep up the Ratnagalla custom,' he said. And so, in her thin slippers and yards of lace and satin, Camilla walked with her new husband down the long rows, partitioned off into separate apartments opening out onto a verandah which ran the length of the building. Men, women and children came out onto this verandah to gaze at the spectacle of the European bride. There was curiosity in their eyes, but it was friendly, not hostile, for the Periya Durai of Ratnagalla was known as a fair and reasonable employer, firm but not unkind.

All the same, seeing these people crowding round to look at her, swamped by the many dark faces and pairs of dark eyes, Camilla was deeply conscious that here, almost on their doorstep, was a different way of life. A small colony carried on an intense, complex and often clamorous existence of its own, with its customs and festivals, its rites of birth, marriage and death. These people were almost as foreign to Ceylon as were the planters themselves, but many of them would never go back to the homes they had left across the narrow straits.

Dinner that evening was a sumptuous affair. Lal had surpassed even his usual excellence, and they sat down to a veritable banquet.

Doña Lucia was in higher spirits than Camilla had ever seen her and, in reminiscent mood, began to tell a story about the first occasion on which she had met Edgar Ballantyne, at a dinner party given by mutual acquaintances. Edgar had been new to the island and had a reputation as a bit of a tearaway, and the strictly reared Portuguese girl had been somewhat alarmed to find herself seated next to him at dinner.

'I did not know what to talk to him about,' she

recalled. 'But there was game of some sort on the menu, and I knew some of the gentlemen had been on a shooting party, so I said, "And did you, sir, shoot this?" thinking it to be a fairly safe topic. And what did he reply? He glared at me, and said, "Why? Isn't it dead?"'

Her laughter trilled out loudly at this recollection, but her family, who had obviously heard this story many times before, merely smiled.

Camilla found herself wondering about the relationship between Ballantyne père and Doña Lucia. Phillip had insinuated that Edgar had married Doña Lucia for her money, and certainly, the da Silva fortune must have helped to finance Ratnagalla. But had he loved her? She had loved him, Camilla was convinced, not simply because she had worn black since the day he died, it was implicit in the way she would sometimes talk incessantly about him, and at other times could not bear his name to be mentioned at all. And surely, only her intense devotion to him could have persuaded her aristocratic Portuguese parents to give their daughter in marriage to an unknown English adventurer.

At last, the long and tiring day came to an end. Instead of the small room which had become home to her since her arrival, Camilla retired to the large master bedroom, splendidly decorated in cream and gold, with an immense four-poster bed which had been laboriously brought up from the da Silva home in Colombo, long ago.

It was a relief to take of the wedding dress and the constricting underclothes, and put on the simple but finely made nightdress of white lawn, extravagantly trimmed with lace. Fanny brushed out Camilla's hair until it fell in loose, silvery waves, framing a face that was suddenly very pale. And then, since there was nothing more she could do for her mistress, and she had no valid excuse for remaining, Fanny retired for the night and Camilla was alone.

The girl stood at the window, looking out at the clear night, and the gardens bathed in moonlight. The sounds of revelry drifted up from the lines, carried on the night air. It was music she remembered vaguely from her childhood, high-pitched and melodic, with the insistent beat of drums in the background. A wedding had taken place and there would be feasting, with as much food as could be eaten, provided by the big house for the occasion. The celebrations would go on half the night. For the Tamils, a wedding was not a hushed, decorous affair, but a splendid and gorgeous event, an excuse for everyone to make merry and forget their drab, workaday lives.

A sound behind her made her turn suddenly, to see Javier in the doorway.

'I'm sorry if I startled you. I did knock, but perhaps you didn't hear me,' he said politely, closing the door behind him.

Camilla unclasped her tightly laced fingers, and endeavoured to smile at him in a manner which was at the same time welcoming and demure.

'I was listening to the music,' she said. 'It reminded me of when I was a child. Odd how a little thing like that can bring back so many memories.'

I am talking too much, she thought, and made a conscious effort to stop babbling. It was difficult, now that he was closer to her, and they were at last alone. She was so terribly aware of him, tall and commanding and masculine, that the strength drained from her limbs and she was bathed in an exquisite weakness, which was delight and longing, inextricably mingled. Now, he would take her in his arms and carry her to the vast, curtained bed, now she would know the touch of his hands and his lips, and to the beating of the Tamil drums, and the wild, convoluted thread of the melody, he would make her his. Camilla closed her eyes. Now . . .

'I came,' said Javier, formally and distinctly, 'to wish you goodnight.'

Her lids flew open again, and she stared at him in uncomprehending astonishment.

'But . . .' she said faintly, 'I don't understand.'

He pointed to a door in the corner of the room, which had escaped her notice.

'That is the connecting door to my dressing-room, where I shall sleep,' he said. 'Although it does have its own door on to the corridor, I shall enter every night by this door. The pretence shall be kept up.'

'The pretence?' she echoed, aware that she was sounding stupid.

'We have been through all this, Camilla,' he said, with icy patience. 'We agreed that ours was to be a marriage of convenience, a business arrangement. You are not going to tell me that you have forgotten that conversation.'

'No,' she said slowly, trying to keep calm whilst everything was reeling about her. 'I have not forgotten. But, forgive me—am I to infer that our relationship is to be entirely platonic?'

'Naturally,' he said coolly. 'If I take a woman to bed, I do *not* regard it as a business arrangement. I regard it as something altogether different.

The sardonic twist was present once more in his smile, as he said, 'You have what many women would consider the best of all possible worlds, Camilla. The security and established position of a married woman, and a husband who will make no demands on you.'

He took her hand and brushed it lightly with his lips, as chastely as if she were a stranger to whom he had just been introduced, and looking down briefly on his bent dark head, Camilla was seized by a wild notion to clasp him to her, to be close to him at all costs, in the frenzied hope that he would be unable to refuse her. But looking into his eyes as he straightened up once more, she saw that they were impassive and unemotional, and that there was no such hope.

So she could only watch, speechless, as he disappeared into the dressing room, closing *that* door very firmly behind him.

At first she felt nothing, a kind of numbness anaesthetised her, as she stared at the door that shut him out of her life, out of the nights she had dreamed they would spend together. Then, very slowly, feeling began to return to her, and she was dazed by the shock of what he had said to her, hurt by his rejection, and ashamed of her own unmitigated and very real desire.

Could he really mean that there was to be nothing at all between them, that they were to spend their whole lives tied together in this travesty of a marriage? She could not believe it. How could he expect it of her, young and warm blooded as she was, to live not only without love, but without the physical expression of love?

Her mind flew back in helpless panic to that conversation in the moonlit garden, when he had spelled out his terms for their marriage. A marriage of convenience— yes, but by that she had taken him to mean a marriage entered into for reasons other than love, expediency, family considerations and so forth. She had not thought he was saying that he and she would never share the same bed. But as she thought, his words came clearly back to her. 'I do not expect, or even desire you to demonstrate any affection for me . . . or to pretend to feelings we both know are absent from the transaction.' It had been plain enough, if she had *wanted* to understand it. Javier was saying that he did not love her, and did not care to make love to a woman for whom he had no desire.

The fact was that she had not wanted to understand those words, had not believed them or taken them seriously. Instead, she had listened to her own heart, confident that when the time came she could sweep aside all such objections. Had he said to her 'I do not intend to make love to you,' she most probably would still have gone ahead with the wedding, out of the same obstinate disbelief. Well, the time had come, and she must now pay for her own foolishness.

Sick at heart, Camilla sank down on to the sumptuous bed. How could she reach him, now? He had closed to her the path she had hoped to tread, the passionate response of her eager and youthful senses. He did not love her; neither did he desire her, so it would appear.

Outside, the music rose to a crescendo of delight, the drums beat themselves to a frenzy, celebrating the wedding night of Camilla da Silva Ballantyne, who lay alone in her palatial bedroom, her hands clenched, her eyes closed tight against the despair that engulfed her.

She did eventually sleep that night, but not until long after the drums were silent and the Tamil revellers were quiet in their quarters. Consequently, she slept late and when she awoke the tea tray was at the side of her bed, where Mohini had left it when she tiptoed in and found the new memsahib still fast asleep.

Camilla sat up, poured her tea and gazed around the unfamiliar room. The scene enacted here last night between herself and her reluctant bridegroom still lingered unpleasantly in her memory, but the bright sunlight cast a more optimistic glow over her dilemma. She could not—would not—accept that his words on the subject were final. Time and youth were on her side, and she did not intend to give him up without a fight. She would love him, enchant him, use any weapon nature had given her to make herself infinitely desirable to him. One day, he will be mine, she vowed passionately.

She rang for Fanny, deciding that it was time she got up. Javier would have been out on his rounds long ago, and whilst no one expected a new bride to be up too early, she did not intend to lie in bed half the day.

Fanny did not answer as promptly as usual so Camilla rang again, and, once more, there was a puzzling silence. At her third ring, after a quite a lengthy pause in between, it was Mohini who appeared.

'Ah, Mohini,' said Camilla. 'Something very strange is happening. I've rung three times for Fanny, and there's no sign of her. Have you seen her this morning?'

'No, Miss Camilla. Maybe she's sleeping. Would you like me to go to her room and see?'

It did not escape Camilla's notice that the girl still addressed her as 'Miss Camilla' even though she was now Mrs Ballantyne. But she was accustomed to hearing the menfolk addressed as 'Mr Javier' and 'Mr Phillip' and her mother-in-law was 'Doña Lucia' to all the staff, so she supposed she might be 'Miss Camilla' for the rest of her life. There was nothing symbolic about it, she told herself, even though she did not truly feel she was Mrs Ballantyne, this morning.

'Please—if you would. It isn't like her to be late,' she said.

Mohini was gone for a few minutes only, and when she returned, she was breathless from running, and her eyes were wide in her distraught face.

'Please come quickly, Miss Camilla!' she gasped. 'Fanny is ill! She's very ill!'

Camilla paused only long enough to shrug on a robe over her nightdress, and thrust her feet into slippers, and then she followed Mohini up the narrow flight of steps to Fanny's little room, set under the steep pitch of the gables.

Fanny lay stretched out on her bed, breathing heavily and painfully. Her eyes were wide open, but glazed, she seemed not to recognise them, nor to know where she was. She was bathed in sweat and running a high temperature. Now and again she tossed from side to side, and moaned a little, as if the effort exhausted her.

Camilla laid a hand on her forehead.

'She's burning up!' she said worriedly. 'What is it, Mohini, do you know?'

The girl shook her head.

'Some kind of fever. It's impossible to tell, there are so many,' she said.

Mistress and maid looked at each other for a moment. Then Camilla seemed to realise that she and she alone was responsible for Fanny, and any action must ensue from her.

'Bring some cold water and a sponge,' she ordered briskly. 'We must try to reduce her temperature. Warn the other servants to keep clear of this room, it could be something infectious. I shall nurse her myself.'

Mohini nodded, and swiftly went to do as she was told. When she returned, she said, 'Doña Lucia sent word that she wishes to see you at once, in the drawing-room.'

'But I can't leave Fanny!' Camilla cried in exasperation. 'She needs attention immediately. Doña Lucia will have to wait.'

'I will look after her until you return,' Mohini said calmly. 'Please—it will be all right. I know what to do.'

Camilla glanced from the young Indian girl to the moaning, heaving figure of the woman on the bed.

'We do not know what it is. It could be dangerous,' she said in a low voice. 'Aren't you afraid?'

'No. I am not afraid,' Mohini said quietly. 'It is best if you go and see Doña Lucia, or she will become very upset.'

Still in her robe, Camilla sped downstairs to the drawing-room, where she found her mother-in-law pacing agitatedly up and down, and Phillip trying ineffectually to calm her. Camilla had the impression that neither of them would have been out of their bedrooms had not the new of Fanny's sickness run through the house like wildfire.

Doña Lucia stopped pacing at the sight of Camilla,

and regarded her with a shocked expression.

'Why, Camilla! You are not dressed!' she exclaimed reprovingly.

'Oh . . . I didn't have time,' Camilla said, drawing her robe more closely around her, as she felt the probing gaze of Phillip's eyes. The opportunity of observing his brother's wife in a state of semi-undress seemed to have rendered him, for once, speechless with delight.

'We must keep up our standards here, or we shall be no better than the natives,' Doña Lucia chided. 'Now, what is this I hear about your serving woman being taken ill?'

'It's true. She's running a high fever and is most unwell,' Camilla said, edging towards the door, anxious to get back to Fanny. 'In fact, I must ask you to excuse me, I have to see to her.'

'Indeed, you must keep right away from her!' Doña Lucia cried. 'You are my son's wife—we cannot have you contracting any disease! No, it is unthinkable!'

Camilla stood her ground.

'I must. Fanny came to Ceylon with me, I've known her all my life, and I can't just leave her to suffer,' she insisted.

Doña Lucia sank into a chair, clasping a hand to her forehead dramatically, as if it was all too much for her to bear.

'I've sent a messenger to fetch Javier from the factory. At least wait until he gets here,' she begged.

'Very well,' Camilla capitulated. She could see that Doña Lucia's nerves were in a state of imminent collapse, but the principle of being responsible for the servants who worked for her was ingrained too deeply in Camilla for her to agree to stay from Fanny. Her maid was ill, in a strange land where no one else cared for her welfare, and Camilla would not leave her to her fate.

In spite of the cold little débâcle in the bedroom the previous night, Camilla was quite incredibly glad to see the tall figure of her husband enter the room. His very presence reassured her, his strength and authority deepened her conviction that he would know what should be done.

He listened in silence as Camilla briefly and succinctly described Fanny's symptoms.

'We need the doctor,' he said decisively, and turning to Phillip, he said, 'Ride into Nuwara Eliya as quickly as you can, and bring Dr Davies back with you. The message will be clearer that way than if we send one of the servants.'

Phillip appeared staggered by the mere notion of such a feat.

'Oh, I say, Javier, old man!' he protested. 'We had a wedding here yesterday, if you remember, and I did imbibe rather freely. I'm in no condition for such a marathon. Give me chance to have some breakfast and take a bath first!'

Javier looked at his brother with swift contempt, taking in the red rims around the blue eyes, and the general bleariness of his expression.

'Never mind. I'll go myself,' he said shortly. 'You would probably fall asleep on horseback.' He turned to Camilla. 'I shall be back with the doctor as soon as I can,' he promised her. 'In the meantime, keep Fanny as cool as possible, and try not to worry.'

'Oh, thank you!' gasped Camilla, tears springing to her eyes. He favoured her with a brief smile, and his hands closed momentarily over hers, and then he was gone.

For the rest of the day, Camilla and Mohini sat at Fanny's bedside, sponging her feverish body, mopping her brow, and whispering words of comfort which they did not know if she could hear. Towards dusk, the tossing and moaning ceased, and Fanny lay quite still, gazing vacuously at the ceiling, while sweat still dripped from her body. Her breathing seemed more laboured until, as night crept on, she was fighting for every breath.

Across the bed, dark and hazel eyes met, with fading hope. Mohini had fetched her bible, and began to read the 23rd psalm, in a tone of quiet resignation.

'Yea, though I walk through the valley of the shadow of death, I will fear no evil . . .'

'No!' Camilla said fiercely. 'No, she shall not die! I won't let her!'

Mohini only smiled sadly, as if her yielding to the inevitable were wiser than Camilla's exhausting and useless battle against it. Fanny seemed to be sinking slowly into an irreversible stupor, it was in vain Camilla sat and chafed her hand to try and obtain some response. The fever had gone, now, taking the woman's strength with it, and she was quite cold. As the moon rose over Ratnagalla, her stertorous breathing faltered, and finally ceased.

'She's dead, Miss Camilla,' Mohini said gently. 'There's nothing more we can do for her.'

Camilla was in her room when Javier came to her. She sat by the window, dry-eyed and composed, her hands neatly in her lap, and the face she raised to him was calm, although it was possible for anyone sufficiently perceptive to discern that she had been crying.

'I am so sorry,' he said. 'I came as quickly as I could, but these things run their course so swiftly.'

'It is not your fault,' she said. 'You did what you could. Thank you for trying.'

'It is at times like this we pay the penalty for our remote situation. However, if it is any comfort to you, the doctor does not think it would have helped had we been able to reach her sooner. He's totally mystified as to the cause of her illness.'

'He doesn't know what it is that killed her?'

'Not precisely. There are so many different kinds of fever, many of which are still unidentified. Their treatment is often a matter of luck and guesswork. We're still in a state of partial ignorance as regards tropical diseases.'

'I know.' Camilla sighed wearily. 'There was something I once read, by the wife of a government official, I don't quite remember who. She said that in India, death was such a cunning hunter that before you know you are ill, you may be ready to become his prey . . . that death, the grave, and forgetfulness may be the work of two days . . .' She shuddered, thinking of all the hundreds of women who had followed their menfolk east to an early grave. 'Fanny had never been ill in her life, to the best of my knowledge. Like your father,' she added, struck suddenly by the comparison.

He gave her a strange look.

'Not exactly. My father did not run a fever. He just died, quite inexplicably. Don't dwell too deeply on it, Camilla. It's part of life in the East, and until we acquire greater knowledge than we now possess, we just have to accept it.'

At the door, he paused and looked back at her, taking in the washed-out pallor of her face, the dark-ringed eyes.

'Get some rest,' he advised. 'The doctor will be staying the night, and he will want to see you in the morning.'

It was decided that since it was impossible to say definitely whether Camilla was the victim of any infection, the safest course would be for her to keep to her room for a few days. Apart from Javier, who came every evening to see how she was, and Mohini, to whom he delegated the task of looking after her, the rest of the household left her strictly alone.

To Camilla, still stricken by grief over Fanny's death, the isolation was welcome. But as time passed, and both she and Mohini appeared to be unaffected, she decided it was time for her to emerge once more into the life of the household.

'Ah, my favourite sister-in-law,' Phillip joked lightly, as she appeared among them for luncheon for the first time since Fanny's death.

Camilla merely smiled sedately and said nothing. She had found him entertaining enough before, but since that morning when he had refused to ride for the doctor, as if the well-being of a servant were of insufficient import to cause him so much exertion, she could not bring herself to feel any affection for him.

'What I am wondering, Camilla, is what you are going to do about a maid?' Helen blurted out tactlessly. 'Lola isn't getting any younger, and it's all she can do to look after mother and myself.'

Lola was a silent, rather sour-faced Portuguese woman who had been with Doña Lucia for many years.

'I don't think I need trouble Lola at all,' Camilla said. 'Mohini is quite capable of looking after me—she's being doing it for the past few days, anyhow. She can be my maid from now on.'

She had not consciously wondered up until that moment how she was going to replace Fanny, but now she had said it, it appeared to be the ideal solution. She was genuinely fond of the girl, who had incurred considerable risk by nursing the sick woman, and what was more, she had promised Lal she would do her best for his daughter. For Mohini, it could only be a step up, from kitchen to lady's maid, and she would have the girl where she could keep an eye on her, and generally promote her welfare.

Helen's lip curled scornfully.

'A native girl for a personal maid!' she declared disdainfully. 'It is not quite the thing, Camilla! That girl already considers herself something special, now she will be quite impossible.'

'Nevertheless,' Camilla said firmly and with great determination, 'that is what I shall do.'

Helen continued to make noises about the unsuitability of the idea, and Phillip said irritably, 'Oh, don't fuss so, Helen! Is it a matter of great importance, who looks after you girls and your frills and fol-de-rols? Besides, Camilla may do as she pleases.'

'Mother won't like it,' Helen said primly. 'You know how she feels about giving the natives ideas above their station.'

'Where is Doña Lucia, by the way?' Camilla asked, adroitly changing the subject, and she saw a wary glance pass between brother and sister.

'Oh, she's not too well,' Helen said evasively. 'The headaches, you know, and she's been a little depressed, as a result of illness in the house.'

Camilla had a notion that all this tiptoeing around the house and speaking in hushed voices whenever Doña Lucia had a headache did not really help. After lunch, she decided to go and see her mother-in-law, and try to cheer her up a little. Then, perhaps, the headache would go away of its own volition. She slipped out into the garden and picked a small bunch of Doña Lucia's favourite roses, thinking their fragrant beauty would delight her, and went up to the other woman's room.

Her tap on the door was answered by Lola, who opened it just a fraction, and peered out at Camilla with the utmost suspicion.

'My mistress is seeing no one,' she said in a surly tone. 'She is not well.'

Over the woman's shoulder, Camilla could see that the room was in semi-darkness, the blinds pulled down to shut out the bright glare of the afternoon. Doña Lucia was prostrate on her bed.

'Who is it, Lola?' she called out weakly.

'It's me, Camilla,' the girl herself said. 'I came to see how you were. I thought perhaps I could sit and talk with you for a while, if you wished.'

Doña Lucia raised herself on one elbow, and as Lola

allowed the aperture to become a little larger, Camilla advanced a couple of steps into the room.

It was like a mausoleum. Everything was in dark, sombre colours, and everywhere, on every table top, dressing table and what-not available, were portraits of Edgar Ballantyne as a young man, in his later years, and at every stage between.

'Yes,' Doña Lucia spoke in a low voice, almost a whisper. 'Handsome, is he not? But when he came to Ceylon, he was nobody. *Nobody!* Whereas I . . .' she paused, and her voice rose an octave as she went on, 'There was a da Silva on one of the caravels commanded by Don Laurenco de Almeida, in 1505, the first Europeans ever to visit Ceylon. That da Silva was related to the kings of Portugal.'

She laughed suddenly, and sat bolt upright. 'I never dreamed they would allow me to marry him. But they did. Why, do you think, was that?'

'Perhaps because you loved him,' Camilla replied quietly.

Doña Lucia began to laugh, soft, hysterical laughter, rocking back and forth, her arms cradled around her own body.

'Better you go!' Lola hissed, and Camilla turned to comply. She had been wrong to come here, her mother-in-law was not fit to receive her, and there was something more than a headache amiss with her.

'Wait!' Doña Lucia cried out, and Camilla, arrested in the doorway, turned back to see that she was now off the bed and on her feet, swaying a little, her face contorted with anger. For the first time, she had noticed the flowers Camilla held in her hand, and it was those which had acted as a catalyst, turning her hysteria to rage.

'How dare you desecrate my garden!' she demanded furiously. 'How dare you! No one is allowed to touch the roses, except I myself! How dare you!'

'I'm . . . I'm sorry,' stammered Camilla, taken aback. 'I thought they would make you feel better. I didn't mean to upset you.'

Doña Lucia was trembling.

'It was a mistake to bring you here!' she said. 'You can do nothing! I thought she would go, once you came, but she is still here, the one they called Anula. I can feel it—she is still here!'

She threw herself on the bed and began to sob violently, and thresh around with her arms. Lola ran to try and restrain her, speaking in low, rapid Portuguese, of which Camilla understood not one word. Her presence, she saw, could only exacerbate the situation, so she left the room and walked quickly down the corridor, her hands gripping the roses so tightly that the thorns pricked her flesh, and blood spotted her dress.

And now, Camilla longed for the down-to-earth, reassuring presence of Fanny to help her through the tangle of emotions which warred and conflicted under this roof. Nothing here was as it seemed to be, and Fanny, she recalled, had said so on the day they arrived at Ratnagalla. 'There's something strange, something I can't quite put my finger on . . .'

Camilla had felt that strangeness quite distinctly in Doña Lucia's room. She had known her mother-in-law was volatile, subject to violent changes of mood, but she had not thought anyone could get so excited and angry over a few flowers. And who was this Anula, of whom she had spoken, whose presence Camilla's arrival was supposed to dispel, but who was 'still here'? It did not make sense.

Mohini might know something, she thought, and when the Indian girl came to help her change for dinner, Camilla said abruptly, 'Who is Anula, Mohini?'

Mohini's expression was startled and wary.

'A bad, a wicked girl,' she exclaimed, shaking her smooth, dark head. 'The Hindu priest who sometimes comes here brought her with him. Some say she was a *deva-dashi*.'

Camilla nodded. She knew that the priest would from time to time appear in the Tamil lines, to conduct any rituals which might be necessary. He was needed because of his working knowledge of Sanskrit, and his understanding of the complicated technicalities of those rites, but he would in no way consider himself responsible for the moral or spiritual welfare of those whom he visited. He was not a father of his flock, as was the Reverend Fielding, such a concept had no place in Hindu belief. Nor was he expected to be celibate or to have a reputation for great virtue. A *deva-dashi*, Camilla knew, was a kind of temple prostitute.

'So the priest brought her. And what happened?'

Mohini gave a little shrug, as if such matters were outside her concern.

'When the priest left, she stayed. There is a temple not far away, in the hills. Once there was a city there, built by invaders from Southern India, long ago, and you can still see the ruins of it, although the temple is the only part of it remaining intact. It is a temple to the God, Shiva, and the Tamils take offerings there—flowers and food. The girl was often to be seen there. She called herself Anula—who knows if that was really her name— after a queen of ancient times, who within seven years married, put on the throne and then poisoned five lovers. The Tamil labourers were all in awe of her. They said she was an incarnation of Parvati, who is the bride of Shiva.'

Camilla frowned deeply, concentrating hard to bring to the surface what little she knew of Hindu mythology. Shiva, the Destroyer, whose cosmic dance was the endless recycling of the universe, and his consort, Parvati, who, in the way of Hindu deities, was also the mother goddess, Durga, and Kali, of the many limbs and terrible visage, a severed head held in her hand . . .

'They are only ignorant peasants, mistress,' Mohini sniffed. 'You know I do not believe in any of this superstition.'

'But *they* do,' Camilla pointed out, 'And presumably, this girl Anula knew they did. She must have exerted considerable influence.'

'They say she used to dance naked before the temple at night, wearing only jewelled anklets and bracelets,' Mohini whispered. Whether she professed to believe in it or not, some memory deep in her consciousness could not resist the imagery, Camilla thought. 'And then, one day, she was gone . . . no one knew how or where she went, but for some time, no one has seen her dance.'

Camilla digested all this, and then said thoughtfully, 'But I don't see what all this has to do with Doña Lucia. She seems to have got it into her head that the girl is still around.'

Mohini hesitated.

'Maybe I should not say this, but . . .' she shook her head. 'No, I cannot.'

'Go on, please,' Camilla urged. 'Nothing you say to me will go beyond this room.'

'Well . . . it is only that Doña Lucia sometimes does not know quite what she is saying. She becomes very distraught, and has to be confined to her room for a while, sometimes for a period of several days.'

'*Confined?*' Camilla did not mistake the overtones of that word. 'What you are trying to say, in the politest possible manner, is that Doña Lucia is slightly deranged,' she said bluntly. 'Is that it?'

Mohini nodded.

'I was little more than a child when I was sent to Colombo, but already there were signs of it. Now, it seems, those times when she is not well are coming closer together, and lasting longer. The mistress is losing her mind, Miss Camilla. Of course, no one will admit as much, but that is why guests are so rarely invited to Ratnagalla.'

And why she had to be married here, instead of in the church at Nuwara Eliya, Camilla realised. She understood, now, why Javier needed a wife, or at least, a mistress of his household. *Of course* no one would admit it, she thought. Such things were generally spoken of in whispers, if at all. Society was offended by, and frightened of mental illness, the insane were locked away in terrible institutions for its protection.

Doña Lucia was far from being in any such category. For much of the time, apart from being excessively nervous, she was as normal as anyone else, but what set this household on edge was the irrationality of her condition, the awareness that at any time the semblance of normality could crumble.

Strangely enough, Camilla was not unduly dismayed by the information she had just received, she only wished she had been told earlier, so that she could temper her behaviour accordingly. But she supposed it was too much to expect Javier to have said, 'My mother suffers from incipient madness, and I need you to run the menage when she is incapable of doing so.' He had told her Doña Lucia's health was suspect, that she was easily upset, and she might have deduced the rest for herself, had she not been so bound up with her own problems.

And Anula? At some time, Camilla presumed, her mother-in-law must have heard the story of the naked temple dancer, and it had preyed on her fevered mind. What connection there was between Anula and herself she failed to see, and perhaps, in view of Doña Lucia's state of mind, she should not expect to do so.

For the next few days, Camilla took over the management of the household completely. Not that she had to worry excessively over it, Lal was unfailingly efficient, and quite unflappable, and a certain respect and understanding was growing up between them. He could not thank Camilla enough for taking Mohini as her maid, and there was nothing he would not do to smooth her path for her. The girl herself was equally ecstatic about her promotion, and worked so diligently that Camilla could not help but congratulate herself on her choice.

If only she could have taken the same pleasure in her marriage. Javier had observed scrupulously and to the letter the terms he had set out on the night of their wedding, and there was no indication that he would deviate from them. In front of the family he was fault-lessly polite to her, away from the gaze of others, it was as if she scarcely existed for him.

Every night, he entered the master bedroom, wished her a cool goodnight, and retired to his dressing room. Sometimes Camilla would attempt to engage him in conversation in the hope of keeping his company for a little while, but he seemed only too anxious to get away from her. She took immense pains with her appearance at all times, and always wore a dress which showed off her beauty at its best for dinner, when, for an hour or so, he would be seated opposite her at the table. The soft glow of the lamps enhanced Camilla's smooth, bare shoulders and played on the silvery curls framing her face, leaving free the long, slim column of her neck. But Javier seemed impervious to the display of his wife's charms, it seemed that she did not present him with the slightest temptation.

She endeavoured to remain calm and pleasant when they did meet. It was far from easy, when every day her love for him, her desire for him grew, and he remained indifferent. But a carping, dissatisfied woman would only drive him further from her, she knew. Patience was her only hope, although there were times when she felt her self-control stretched to a point where it would surely snap, like a too-taut wire.

One afternoon, Camilla was surprised to find that her husband had returned to the house for afternoon tea, which he was taking with Mac, the engineer, and another younger man, blond and athletically, if rather heavily built. Both these men were formally attired, Mac, for once, free of machine oil, for tea at the big house was an important event in the life of estate employees.

All three men rose to their feet as Camilla came out onto the verandah, and Javier said, 'Piet, let me introduce you to my wife. Camilla, this is Piet van der Viert, my assistant manager. He has been back to Amsterdam on leave, and only returned to Ratnagalla late last night.'

'Delighted,' said the young Dutchman, bowing over Camilla's hand. 'Rumours of the new Mrs Ballantyne's charm and beauty are flying around Nuwara Eliya, and have even penetrated as far as Colombo, and I see they are not exaggerated.'

Camilla smiled.

'You are very kind, Mr van der Viert, but these rumours are mere speculation, as no one has seen me,' she observed.

'Dr Davies has, and the Reverend Fielding has, and they are men, after all,' van der Viert said exuberantly.

They all seated themselves, and Camilla poured the tea. It was the nearest thing to a social occasion she had known at Ratnagalla, and she was enjoying it. To see admiration on a man's face was balm to a woman whose husband steadfastly refused to have anything to do with her.

'I'm riding over to Hazelgrove tomorrow,' Javier informed his assistant. 'Now that you are back, I think the estate can spare me for a day.' Turning to Camilla, he said, 'This is an estate which adjoins Ratnagalla. The owner's coffee crop has failed, and he's selling up. I'm thinking of buying, if the price is right. Would you care to come with me and look it over?'

'I should love to!' Camilla exclaimed, with intense

pleasure. She checked herself, thinking that perhaps her response was a little too ecstatic, but neither of the other two men seemed surprised. After all, the young Ballantynes were virtually still on honeymoon.

'I must go over there before the monsoon makes it difficult, if not impossible,' Javier said. 'And we cannot have it said that I sequester you away here and permit no one to see you, can we?'

There was a touch of sarcastic irony in his voice which diminished Camilla's happiness a little, but she refused to allow herself to be entirely downcast. She was to have a whole day with Javier, away from Doña Lucia's hysterics, Helen's sulks, and Phillip's insidious suggestiveness. Just the two of them, and the miles of lush, splendid Ceylonese hill country. She tried not to stake too much on this single day, knowing that most probably, at the end of it, her relationship with Javier would be much the same as it was now, but it was difficult not to rejoice at the prospect.

CHAPTER
FIVE

THE day began with breakfast for the two of them at an hour earlier than Javier usually observed, for to make the trip in one day, he told her, they would need an early start. Dawn was just breaking as they rode out from Ratnagalla, and the rows of tea bushes stood silent sentinels, while swathes of mist wrapped the peaks in mystery.

Camilla did not speak, and neither did Javier. For her, his presence was sufficient, and forced chatter would only have intruded on the quiet companionship they shared. For him, she sensed, every morning in Ceylon was the renewal of a personal miracle, the repledging of a deep and continuing love for the land where he was born. This they could share, she thought, in this, if in nothing else, they were united. And it was as if no words were needed for each of them to know it.

She knew at once when they reached Hazelgrove, for all around them were the stunted and dying coffee trees in the final stages of disease. Javier picked a leaf, and showed Camilla the rust-red spots on its underside.

'This is the killer,' he told her. '*Hemileia vastatrix*, the coffee blight. They tried, and are still trying everything to combat it, but nothing seems to work. The only answer, for those who have enough capital to tide them over, is to dig up the trees completely and re-plant with a different crop. Carstairs, who owns Hazelgrove, doesn't have that kind of backing, so he's selling out.'

'But the trees are being uprooted, nonetheless,' Camilla said, and indeed, the only activity on this estate was that of the elephants which were being employed to pull up the trees.

'Indeed,' Javier said sombrely. 'The branches are stripped and exported to England—to make legs for tea tables. It's the final ignominy for a coffee planter, but at least that way he does recoup something from his investment.'

When they arrived at the Carstairs' bungalow, word of their approach must have gone ahead of them, for the planter and his wife were out on the verandah waiting to meet them. Theirs was a much smaller and less imposing residence than the house at Ratnagalla, but pleasant and comfortable, with wistaria climbing the walls. Mrs Carstairs was delighted that Camilla had come along with her husband, and whisked her inside to freshen up before lunch.

'It must be dreadful for you to have to leave this place,' the girl said with ready sympathy, but her hostess gave a cheerful shrug.

'Oh, I shan't be sorry, in a way,' she said. 'Since all this trouble began, we've just had to sit here and watch helplessly as our money drained away. It will be a relief to sell up and make a clean break.'

Her husband echoed these sentiments over lunch. 'We're hoping to go to the Malay states,' he said. 'Things there are just opening up, and we'll see what we can find.'

The two men retired to talk business, and the women strolled around the garden.

'This house is the only thing I shall miss,' Mrs Carstairs remarked. 'I suppose if your husband buys Hazelgrove he will put a manager in, but I should like to think of a family growing up here, as mine did.'

Looking around the garden, bright with flowers and somnolent with the buzz of insects, Camilla had a sudden fancy to live here herself. Compared with Ratnagalla it was modest, but how lovely it would be to live here, just herself and Javier and a small staff, away from the overloaded atmosphere of that other house. Closing her eyes, she heard the imaginary cries of children playing, children she would never have, and all at once she was sick with despair and longing.

Mrs Carstairs took Camilla's arm, and looked with concern into the pale and wistful face.

'My dear, are you all right?' she asked gently. 'It is a little soon, I know, but I swear when I was carrying my eldest, I knew before the month was out.'

'Oh, no, it's nothing like that,' Camilla said hastily. 'I'm perfectly all right.'

It would be ironic, she thought, if this nice woman were to start a rumour circulating that the new Mrs Ballantyne was pregnant already, when the truth was that her husband resolutely avoided her bed.

'All the same, I think we shall sit on the verandah and have some tea,' Mrs Carstairs said, obviously not entirely convinced. And there they were a little while later, when the two men emerged from their discussions, smiling broadly.

'I think we should toast the new owner of Hazelgrove with something more than tea!' Mr Carstairs declared. 'Dorothea, is there any champagne?'

'Tea will be quite sufficient, as my wife and I have a long ride back ahead of us,' Javier smiled. He looked quietly pleased as if the agreement they had reached was most satisfactory.

'Well, I suppose tea is apt enough, since that is what you will be growing here,' the other man said. 'I worked as an assistant manager on a tea estate before I bought this place, and if I'd had a clue what was coming, I'd have stuck to tea. But there's no need to feel you must leave immediately. Stay the night—we can easily put you up.'

'Thank you, but we must get back to Ratnagalla tonight,' Javier insisted politely. 'My assistant is only just back from leave, and isn't quite *au fait* with all that's happened in his absence, and I don't like to pitch him straight in and leave him to it.'

Camilla wondered if that were the only consideration which made it necessary for them to leave today, or if it had occurred to Javier that staying the night at Hazelgrove would undoubtedly entail sharing a room with his wife. He would go to any lengths, she thought bitterly, to avoid that necessity.

The swift, tropical dusk closed in around them as they rode back the way they had come. Adam's Peak stood out clearly on the skyline, dwarfing the lower hills, and the moon rose clear and golden in the black velvet sky.

Javier was totally at ease in this exotic and darkly beautiful landscape. To him it was home, and always had been, but still he was conscious of its inherent mystery, of the heavy weight of legend and history weighing down this tear-shaped island at the southernmost tip of the Indian subcontinent. As they rode, he talked easily and without restraint about Ceylon's fascinating heritage.

'Did you know that Ceylon is supposed to have been the Garden of Eden?' he said. 'Sinbad the sailor was reputed to have made landfall here, and it was here King Solomon was said to have obtained gems for the Queen of Sheba.'

'I find it quite believable,' Camilla breathed. 'But where did you learn all this?'

'Oh, there's more,' he told her. 'A knowledge of Sanskrit is the key to much of Ceylon's legend and history, and that I learned from my father, who was a Sanskrit scholar. Does that surprise you,' he asked, observing the sudden up-tilt of Camilla's head, 'that a rough planter should have a thirst for the knowledge of the East?'

'Who is the rough planter—your father or yourself?' she could not resist asking, and he laughed with genuine appreciation.

'Why, both, of course. I had the benefit of a European

education, but my roots are here. As a child, I was steeped in stories of Vijaya, the first king of Ceylon, founder of the Sinha, or Lion race, who married the demon princess, Kuveni; of Kasyapa, who ruled from the rock fortress of Sirigiya, where he lived in terror of his own misdeeds, and finally killed himself. The history of Ceylon is a fabulous annal, full of magnificent cities, all manner of kings, from benevolent Buddhist rulers to complete megalomaniacs, Tamil invasions and savage, inter-familial feuds. It's like standing at the end of a dark corridor, with flashes of light here and there to illumine the shadows, but so long you can't see the other end. It stretches back to the dawn of recorded time.'

He looked down at Camilla's upturned face. 'Am I boring you with all this?' he inquired with sudden reserve.

'Far from it, I'm fascinated, and wish you would tell me more,' she said eagerly.

But he seemed to withdraw from her all at once.

'Some other time. We should watch our footing here, it's tricky riding by night,' he said abruptly. Riding behind him, Camilla thought that this strange, stubborn, complex man she had married had just revealed another facet of himself, hitherto unsuspected, and she wished he would let her into his life, so she could truly understand him in all the diversity of his thoughts and aspirations. But every time he opened the door to her a little, she found it swiftly closed again in her face. And so it was now, as they continued the rest of the way to Ratnagalla in silence.

As they passed the small bungalow where Piet van der Viert lived, something made Camilla glance backwards, to where the blond Dutchman stood half-concealed in the shadows of his verandah. A dark shape flitted across the expanse of ground which separated the big house from the assistant manager's accommodation—the shape of a woman in European dress, and as Camilla watched the shadowy forms of the man and the woman merged in an embrace. Even in the darkness, the thin body and quick, terse, gliding footsteps were unmistakable. It was Helen Ballantyne.

Camilla looked quickly away from them, and gazed steadily at her husband's back. But he was looking straight ahead, and had not seen this brief but telling exchange.

So Helen was having an affair, or at least was romantically involved with van der Viert. Doña Lucia would disapprove most thoroughly if she knew, Camilla was sure, but she was equally sure that *she* was not going to be the one to give away Helen's secret. The assistant manager had been away for some time, so it must be a long-standing attachment, for the girl had gone quite readily into his arms, as if it were nothing new to her.

The aristocratic Portuguese matron, whose parents had so surprisingly permitted her to marry the eccentric, untitled Englishman would not give her only daughter to her son's assistant, a mere employee, with no background to speak of, and no money beyond his salary.

Helen was avid for marriage, and had hinted more than once that her mother was deliberately blocking her chances. Certainly, it was hard to see how the girl was ever going to meet any prospective suitors when she did not go anywhere, and no one was invited to the house. Camilla decided she would speak to Javier as tactfully as she could, and without mentioning anything of what she had seen. Perhaps they could consider entertaining a little, or if that would be too much for Doña Lucia, perhaps she, Camilla, could chaperon Helen on a visit to Colombo.

As she had been afraid, the day they had spent together changed nothing between Camilla and Javier. It was just a golden day for her to treasure in her memory, and she was beginning to lose the tenacious faith she had clung to when she married him, that one day he would love her, beginning to believe that her hopes and all her efforts were doomed to failure, and she would never be any more to him than she was now.

'If you love him, he will destroy you,' Fanny had said. The marriage was in its early days, but already that dour prophecy was coming true. He was destroying her, slowly, inch by inch, taking away that blithe, youthful confidence in herself as a woman which had been hers when she first came to Ceylon. How much more of this could she stand, in the months, years that stretched ahead, and if she stayed with him, how much of the bright, determined, adventurous Camilla would be left, after his stony indifference had done its work?

And yet . . . sometimes, when he spoke to her, he seemed to open up as he did to no one else. There was much that they had in common, an outlook on life that was broadly the same, a belief in individual endeavour, an interest in the culture and history of Ceylon, a deep love for Ratnagalla and a desire to increase its prosperity. Surely, they could build a marriage on these solid foundations, especially if they had children to follow them.

If only you would let me love you, she thought, her eyes seeking out the tall figure on the verandah, gazing out silently into the night.

Dinner was over, and Camilla felt she simply could not endure another evening of Doña Lucia's edginess, which made every chance comment the wrong thing to have said, and Helen's covert clock-watching as she urged the evening away so that she could sneak across to Piet van der Viert's bungalow. Excusing herself, she went up to her room and rang for Mohini to help her change.

'It's early, Miss Camilla,' the girl said, concern in her voice. 'Are you not feeling well?'

'Quite well, thank you, Mohini, just a little tired. Perhaps I shall read for a while and then go to bed. You can go now. I shan't need you again tonight.'

But she was not tired, she discovered once she was alone, nor did she really want to read. Restlessly, she paced the bedroom, aware that if she went to bed now she would be awake half the night.

A tap on the bedroom door disturbed her, and her heart began to pound as she wondered if it might be Javier.

'Come in,' she called, puzzled, for he usually simply gave a brief knock and came straight in. But it was Phillip who entered, and Camilla's eyes widened with surprise.

'Phillip, what are you doing here?' she asked coolly. 'Did you not hear me say that I was retiring for the night?'

'I heard you,' he rejoined, 'but it was so early, I could not really believe that you were tired. I thought you might appreciate a little company.'

'Are you out of your mind?' Camilla said sharply. 'You cannot just walk into a lady's bedroom like that, unless that lady happens to be your wife. What if Javier should walk in and find you here?'

'Javier will not be coming up yet, and you know it,' he said casually. 'Besides, what if he did? We are doing nothing improper, only talking.'

'That isn't the point,' Camilla retorted.

'What is the point then, sister?' he asked, laying heavy stress on the last word.

'The point is that you should not be here,' Camilla was beginning to get angry, and her eyes glittered. She was wearing nothing but her thin, lacy night shift, and his immodest scrutiny embarrassed her. Swiftly, she walked across to the door, and held it open. 'Goodnight, Phillip.'

He shrugged and strolled across to the door, and she gave a small sigh of relief, thinking that this unpleasant little crisis was over. But instead of making his exit, he closed the door firmly again, and pinned Camilla against the wall, a hand on either side of her shoulders, so that to escape would have involved her in an undignified struggle.

'Come on, now,' he said. 'Don't tell me you object to a little sport. You're a very beautiful girl, and I'm not a cold fish, like my brother. Or shall we say, I don't share his predilection for the native women.'

Camilla forgot his unwanted proximity, and the uncomfortable position in which he had her pinned.

'His what?' she demanded, looking up urgently into his face.

'Didn't you know?' Phillip said, leering down at her. 'You should ask him one day about the Tamil girl he keeps. Or perhaps better not. Memsahibs are traditionally supposed to turn a blind eye to such liaisons.'

'The one they call Anula,' she said slowly, the final piece of the puzzle slotting into place with an awful certainty.

'So you do know?' he said. 'There you are, then—what's sauce for the gander, the goose doesn't need to be left out of, to paraphrase an old saying. Dazzling creature, Anula, if you go for that type, but I don't. You are more my style.'

His knee was pressing urgently into the softness of her thigh, and the smell of alcohol on his breath reminded her of how much he habitually drank during and after dinner. She struggled then, but too late, his mouth was greedily forcing itself on hers, and his hands groping wildly over her body. Desperately she tried to turn her head away, but he was strong and half-crazed with drink and lust, and her struggles were futile.

The soft click of the door opening was lost on them in the turmoil, and Javier must have stood there for fully half a minute, watching them, his face dark with disgust, before they became aware of his presence.

Phillip sheepishly released Camilla from his unwelcome grasp, and she fell limply against the wall, her hands seeking vainly to straighten her ruffled night shift and tousled hair.

'Didn't mean any harm, old man,' Phillip muttered, taken aback by the cold fury in his brother's eyes. Javier took hold of his brother by the lapels of his coat, and hoisted him unceremoniously to the door.

'I'm fully aware that you've had too much brandy to be responsible for your actions,' he said contemptuously. 'If you were sober, I might fight you. As it is, I've only this to say. If I ever again find you mauling my wife about, I shall horsewhip you. Now—get out.'

He gave Phillip a none too gentle push out into the corridor, and slammed the door behind him.

Camilla was on the verge of offering her husband her heartfelt thanks for his timely arrival, and for rescuing her from Phillip's clutches, but she held her breath as she saw the cold, unrelieved scorn of his expression as he turned to her.

'I must ask you to refrain from entertaining my brother in your bedroom,' he said icily.

She gasped.

'You think I invited him here—that I make a habit of doing so?' she asked. incredulously.

He advanced towards her, slowly and purposefully, and she shrank against the wall, conscious of fear for the first time.

'Are you going to tell me he forced his way in?' he demanded angrily.

'No . . .' Camilla admitted. 'But . . .'

'No, indeed!' he said furiously. 'Because you enjoyed his attentions, did you not? In my own house, under my very nose, you were behaving like a whore! Very well— if that is the kind of treatment you desire!'

Before she had the faintest inkling of what he was going to do, he had seized her by one arm, his fingers biting into her flesh, whilst his free hand gripped the bodice of her night shift and tore it in one swift, vicious action from neck to navel. As the thin lace ripped easily, leaving a jagged tear that exposed Camilla's tender flesh, she screamed instinctively. Grimly, he ignored her cries, swept her into his arms, strode across the room and flung her on to the bed.

The weight of his body forced her down into the enveloping softness of the bed, and Camilla stopped screaming as she looked up into his face, gazing down at her with a new intentness. The hard, unsmiling mouth came down on hers, and there was no tenderness in the hands that explored her body, but she was beyond caring. He was here, in her arms, her hands closed possessively at the back of his neck, pushing up into the thick, dark hair, and she gave herself to his touch and his kisses, without reserve.

She wanted it to go on forever, but it lasted only a few delirious moments before he tore himself free of her embrace, none too gently.

'No, damn you!' he cursed angrily, putting the length of the room between them. He stood with his back to her, leaning against the window, his breath coming heavily in great gasps as if he were being torn in two by an indefinable pain.

Camilla struggled to a sitting position amongst the pillows, pulling the tattered remnants of her shift around her.

'But why, Javier?' she said quietly. In that brief, tempestuous embrace, he had been almost hers, and the sweet triumph running in her veins made all the anger and indignity worthwhile. For that moment, for whatever reason, he had wanted her, and that was undeniably between them, no matter where they went from here.

'I told you,' he said, 'that this was to be a marriage in name only.'

'Yes. You told me,' she said. 'But just then, you wanted to make love to me.'

He turned towards her, once more calm and infuriatingly unreachable.

'You call that making love?' he said dismissively. 'No, Camilla. Most assuredly, it would have been an experience you would not have enjoyed.'

Enjoy it or no, it was preferable to the aloof indifference he had hitherto displayed towards her, she thought fiercely. It was at least a response, albeit a violent one.

'All the same,' she said stubbornly, 'you wanted me.'

He said, 'Don't read too much into it. I was angry when I came in and found you writhing about with Phillip, that's all.'

'I was writhing about, as you put it, trying to get away from him!' she cried furiously, angry tears springing to her eyes.

'Very well. I am prepared to accept that, and also to apologise for my reaction. It was unpardonable, and I am sorry. Will that do?'

His retreat into a sardonic neutrality hurt and enraged her more than his violent and spontaneous fury ever could. She jumped to her feet, clutching the torn lace across her breasts.

'No, it will not do!' she retorted. 'What right have you to come storming in here, behaving like a wronged and jealous husband? Even if I had been entertaining Phillip out of choice, would that have been so entirely unexpected in the circumstances? What am I supposed to do, Javier, when you insist that we live apart?'

'You are supposed to conduct yourself in a proper and seemly manner, according to the agreement we made,' he said stonily. 'It is not my fault if you cannot control your desires. My God!' he exclaimed suddenly, with an amused wryness, 'England is full of prim, virtuous women who faint if their husbands so much as look at them, and when I send for one of these blushing virgins, look what happens!'

A hot flush of shame spread over the ivory skin of

Camilla's face and neck. She did not see why she should stand here and let herself be accused in this way, after what she had learned about him so short a time before.

'So it is unpermissible for me to want a real husband, and children of my own,' she said bitterly, 'but no doubt it is all very right and proper and understandable for you to satisfy your desires with your Tamil mistress!'

His brows rose, and he paused, surveying Camilla's angry, trembling figure.

'Who told you that? Phillip, I suppose,' he said resignedly.

'Does it matter who told me?'

'No, not really,' he said, totally in charge of the situation once again. 'If you find the situation intolerable you can always go back to your grandmother and tell her that it didn't work. But if you decide to stay here, Camilla, you stay on my terms, and those I have made abundantly clear. Now, put on your robe, and let us have no more of this nonsense.'

Alone, Camilla surrendered to the wild, emotional tempest within her. She wept for shame at her own longing, from hurt at his emphatic rejection, but most of all, out of a bitter jealousy, because now she knew why he did not want her.

Another woman already had what Camilla wanted most in the world—his love. A woman whom he could neither marry nor acknowledge openly, but whom he loved, nonetheless. The Tamil temple dancer, whom the priest had brought with him, and who, according to Mohini, had mysteriously disappeared again. But she had not gone. Doña Lucia, who knew of her son's liaison with Anula, and had hoped that Camilla could entice him away from her and back to his legitimate life, his duty to continue the da Silva line, sensed her all-pervasive influence.

Somewhere, Javier had a love-nest where he kept Anula secreted away, where he met her stealthily and made love to her. Where, Camilla wondered, and when? During the long, warm afternoons, when he was supposedly out on his rounds or working hard at the accounts in his office? Camilla buried her face in her pillow to hide the sound of her sobs. To be married to him and not to have his love was torment enough. To know that he belonged, in his heart, to another woman, was intolerable.

She sat up and dried her eyes. Intolerable? That was the word her mind had used, but she must strike it out. This was something she had to bear, because the alternative was not to be considered.

'You can go back to your grandmother and tell her it didn't work,' he had said. And leave him, and never see him again, her own thoughts added. No! Camilla's heart cried out in refusal. That she really could not bear. Her pride was in the dust, she admitted, if it allowed her to stay with a man who treated her this way.

Her chin went up. Would that really be pride she was displaying if she walked out and left him? Or would it be simply defeat, an open admission of failure?

'Come now, child,' she seemed to hear her grandmother's voice, infusing fresh spirit into her. 'You will not be the first Anglo-Indian wife to discover her husband has a native mistress. Fight it, Camilla. If you love him, he is worth fighting for.'

Camilla stood up, and removing the torn night shift, screwed it up into a ball and let it fall to the ground. She would stay at Ratnagalla, yes, but what she could not do was to remain in this room all night, suffocated by the emotions that had been unleashed in it. Swiftly and silently, she began to dress, struggling with the hooks and buttons, without Mohini's help. Finally, dressed in her riding habit and boots, she crept downstairs and let herself out of the sleeping house, into the bright, moon-blanched, spirit-haunted Ceylonese night.

She sped quickly through the gardens down to the

stables, and saddled up her horse with deft and unhesitating hands. Then she was mounted and riding off alone, with the breeze blowing her hair.

The route she followed took her the way she had come on the day she arrived at Ratnagalla. Through the neat terraces of tea bushes, ghostly without the brightly clad labourers who inhabited them throughout the day, the wind stirring the leguminous shade trees planted to protect the young crops from the heat of the daytime sun. On she rode, a solitary dog barking as she passed through the sleeping Sinhalese village.

Here, instead of carrying on into the long valley, she veered right, and found herself plunging into the jungle. Thick, lush vegetation made the going difficult, and the tall trees blotted out the moonlight, leaving horse and rider in an impenetrable blackness, fraught with obstacles.

After several minutes of this, Camilla realised that it had been a little foolhardy of her to come this way, into unknown jungle, alone at night. She dismounted and picked her way carefully, leading her horse, and was about to turn and endeavour to retrace her steps when a glimmer of light ahead led her irresistibly on. She was approaching a clearing.

As the jungle thinned out, Camilla caught her breath, for once, here in the forest, people had lived. Here were the remains of buildings, a broken archway, an area of paving, a wall with intricate frescoes carved on it, all half buried in tangled vegetation as the jungle irrevocably took the remains of the long-dead civilisation back to itself. This, she thought, fascinated, must be the ruined Tamil city Mohini had spoken of, left by those invaders of ancient times.

Leaving her horse tethered to a tree, Camilla went on towards the ruins, pausing to inspect here and there a part of a wall, with smiling, curvaceous maidens still dancing across it in stone, a column entwined with amply-endowed goddesses and splendid gods, locked forever in petrified embrace.

At the far side of the clearing Camilla could see the temple of Shiva, which, as Mohini had said, was the only part of the ancient city left standing in its entirety. Under the moonlight, its stone columns gleamed white, and the carvings stood out sharp and clear. On the ground before it were bowls of fruit, food and flowers, left by the Tamil labourers who had walked through the dense jungle to make their devotions here.

And as she drew nearer to it, mesmerised by the strange effects of the moonlight playing on these centuries-old ruins, and the insidious, encroaching jungle, Camilla became aware that she was not alone here tonight. A woman sat cross-legged in the lotus position, gazing straight ahead of her as if in a trance of delight. Camilla stopped dead, about a hundred yards from the temple and the seated figure. Whether the woman had seen her or not was impossible to tell, for if she had, she gave no indication of it. Slowly, with intense, inward-looking deliberation, she rose to her feet and began to dance.

She was quite naked, except for silver ornaments around her wrists and ankles, and a cloak of night black hair that flowed almost to her waist, but the cool night air appeared to concern her not at all, she was oblivious to everything but the dance she performed. The movements of her hands, arms and legs were intricate and stylised, the poses identical to those of the goddesses frozen in stone all around her. At this distance, her face was only two immense, kohl-ringed eyes and a vermillion slash of a mouth in a smooth, oval face, but her every gesture proclaimed that she was beautiful and proud of her beauty. A swift jerk of her head tossed aside the cloud of hair to reveal the satin perfection of her body as, before the temple of Shiva, langorous and sensual, the bride of Shiva danced. This was Parvati, smiling and benign, dancing in celebration, a woman possessed by love.

Around Camilla, the night hummed, the stars moved implacably in their paths, and the entire Hindu pantheon of gods became real and alive, filling the air with their presence. She herself was overcome by a strange ecstasy, she was replete, then overflowing with a power and excitement which were too great for her to contain. She sank to the ground, her bent head almost touching the grass, her eyes closed. Before she briefly lost consciousness, or transcended self onto a different plane of existence, she was aware of a musical tinkle of bracelets, and a whiff of ambergris.

Camilla came round to a sensation of cold and cramp, she sat up slowly and rubbed her hands together. She was quite alone, the temple was just stones, the stars were unwinking and remote, and the air was still. She supposed it had been so all along, but she had had what she could only describe as a mystical experience.

And it was all due to that woman dancing, the woman who could only be the one called Anula. The woman her husband loved. Camilla had felt the sheer, sensuous power and energy that emanated from her person, the potency of it had left her momentarily senseless. No wonder the Tamil labourers were convinced of her divinity. No wonder Javier loved her with such passion that there was no room in his life for anyone other than her.

Slowly, Camilla stumbled to her feet and made her way back to where she had left her horse. As she led the animal carefully through the jungle, she began to recover her composure. Anula was wholly human, she was in no doubt about that. What had happened had taken place only in her own mind. But the woman who danced had the power to release the imagination of those who watched her, and in her mind, Camilla had seen Shiva's consort dancing.

She was glad to be out of the tangled trees, and riding back again through the village, back to Ratnagalla. She saw to her horse and ran swiftly up the path between the lawns to the house.

But even then, the events of that strange night were not over, for hurrying across the balustraded terrace to the verandah, she collided full tilt with Helen, who was slinking in like a shadow. Neither of them had expected to encounter anyone else at this hour, and they both recoiled with a start.

'Heavens, you made me jump!' Helen accused in a low, angry voice. 'Whatever are you doing out at this hour?'

'I couldn't sleep, so I went for a ride,' Camilla explained, and her sister-in-law regarded her suspiciously.

'At night? You must be mad. What does Javier think to your riding around in the dark, alone?'

'He doesn't know. He's asleep,' Camilla said, trusting that at this hour, what she had said must surely be true.

'I don't believe a word of this!' Helen cried, with the beginnings of hysteria. 'You were spying on me, weren't you? Admit it!'

'Hush, unless you want to waken the entire household!' Camilla admonished, drawing the other girl into the shelter of the verandah. 'I was *not* spying on you. There would have been no point, since I already know about your meetings with Mr van der Viert. I saw you that night when Javier and I came back from Hazelgrove.'

Helen clapped a hand over her mouth to stiffle a cry, and Camilla said reassuringly, 'It's all right. No one else knows, and they won't find out from me.'

'You mean, you aren't going to tell my mother?' Helen said incredulously.

'No. I may be wrong, but I don't feel it's any of my business to interfere. But Helen, you should ask yourself if what you are doing is right, or even sensible.'

'I don't care any more!' Helen burst out, defiantly. 'Look at me—I'm twenty-two, and I'm not a beauty, as you are. My youth is passing, and I'm shut away up here, and no one will ever marry me. My mother has set her face against the idea of my marrying.'

'Perhaps she does not want to lose you,' Camilla suggested, but Helen shook her head.

'No, she has never been passionately attached to me in that way. Javier was always her favourite, right from when we were children. You'd think she would seize any chance to get me settled, but she won't even give me the opportunity to meet any young men.'

Camilla sighed. 'It does seem strange,' she confessed. 'I've suggested that we have one or two small dinner parties, but . . .'

'I know. She said, "Camilla, my dear, you know I cannot stand having the house full of noisy people. It gives me a headache".'

That was virtually word for word what Doña Lucia had said, Camilla had to agree. She said, 'I suggested that you and I went on a trip to Colombo together, but she said to wait until after the monsoon, as it was often not possible to get back beyond Nuwara Eliya in the rains.'

'And after the monsoon, there will be another excuse,' Helen said resignedly. 'It surprises me that you bother on my account, Camilla. I haven't been particularly pleasant to you.'

This was true, but Camilla was only too ready to forget it, and with a wave of her hand, she consigned it all to the past.

'Oh, that doesn't matter. Are you in love with Piet van der Viert, Helen?'

'No,' Helen Ballantyne said bluntly. 'I am not. Does that shock you? Piet is here, and he wants me, or at least, he needs a woman and I am the only European woman available. I have certain needs which are never likely to be fulfilled by marriage, and he satisfies those needs. We fill a space in each other's lives, and I can't see how that harms anyone.'

In the privacy of her room, Camilla thought over what her sister-in-law had said, and in all honesty, she could not see that it harmed anyone, either. Most respectable married women would have condemned a single girl for taking a lover, without even the decent excuse of romantic illusions. But Camilla was not a respectable matron, she was simply another woman whose affections were not returned, whose natural desires were thwarted, and from deep, personal experience, she knew how the other girl felt. If Helen could find solace, happiness even, in the arms of her brother's assistant manager, who was she to stand in her way?

CHAPTER
SIX

THE atmosphere at Ratnagalla was very strained the next day. Helen, still not altogether sure that Camilla meant what she said about not betraying her secret to Doña Lucia, kept casting suspicious glances at her. Phillip studiously refused to meet Camilla's eyes at all. Doña Lucia, who was intensely sensitive to the slightest change of mood in those around her, was as nervous and jumpy as a cat, and kept accusing everyone else of behaving strangely.

Camilla did not see her husband at all until he came into her room while Mohini was helping her to dress for dinner.

Whilst she had said not a word to anyone about her midnight ride, and her experiences in the ruined city, Camilla could not get the episode out of her mind. She was intrigued to know more about the rites attached to the worship of Shiva, and was attempting to find out a little from Mohini. But the girl only shook her head and strenuously denied any knowledge of such things.

'I am a good Christian, Miss Camilla,' she said indignantly. 'I don't have anything to do with those heathen activities.'

The door to the dressing room was slightly ajar, and Javier, who must have overheard this conversation, strolled nonchalantly in. Both women stiffened at his entrance, Camilla felt Mohini's hands falter on the hooks at the back of her dress, and wondered why she should be ill at ease in Javier's presence.

'You cannot really dismiss a culture going back three thousand years as heathenish nonsense, Mohini,' he said, with a slight smile in her direction. 'Of course, the Tamil labourers are simple, uneducated people, and their religious practices reflect that simplicity. But if you read the ancient Vedic writings, and follow the Way of Knowledge, you will discover a deep and sophisticated philosophy.'

The girl's hands seemed suspended helplessly over her mistresses shoulders, and edging her gently out of the way, Javier proceeded to hook up his wife's dress with casual efficiency, whilst she sat turned to stone, pretending that the touch of his hands on the nape of her neck did not disturb her at all.

Completing his self-imposed task, he recited quietly a few lines of flawless Sanskrit, and Mohini trembled visibly, the refined self-control which governed her life threatening to give way.

'Excuse me,' she gulped, and rushed blindly from the room.

Camilla gazed after her in amazement, and then looked at her husband, reflected in the mirror in front of her.

'I've never seen her like that before,' she said. 'Whatever was it you said to upset her so?'

He gave a shrug. 'Oh, that? It was a prayer from the Upanishads, that was all. "Lead me from non-being to being. Lead me from darkness to light. Lead me from death to immortality,"' he translated fluently. 'I think what upset her was the fact that I reminded her how deep her roots are, although she will not admit it.'

He offered Camilla his arm.

'Let us go down to dinner together, like an amicable married couple,' he suggested dryly. The look Camilla gave him was quite unfathomable, but she answered him steadily enough.

'I'm not ready. I still have to put on my pearls.'

'These?' Javier picked up the da Silva pearls from where they lay on the dressing table, and made to fasten them around Camilla's neck, but she jumped up and moved quickly away from him, as if his touch would burn her.

'I can manage, thank you,' she said.

'Of course you can't manage this fiddly, sixteenth-century clasp when you can't see what you're doing,' he said firmly. 'Stand still, Camilla, and don't be silly. I promise not to attack you again. Or have you now decided you would rather I didn't touch you at all?'

His voice was silky, and his hands lingered ever so lightly on her shoulders as he fastened the necklace. Camilla stood rigid, wondering miserably why he should take it into his head deliberately to torment her in this way. She thought of Anula, dancing sensuously, the silver bracelets tinkling as she moved, the cloud of black hair veiling the satin darkness of her skin. Had he spent the afternoon in her arms and, every conceivable desire assuaged, did he now feel free to subject his wife to an exquisitely cruel humiliation?

She turned towards him, her head high. The young and love-sick woman who was Camilla might be longing for him, and prepared to accept any crumb of affection he tossed her way, but Colonel Sumter's grand-daughter had had enough.

'Since you mention it, yes, I would prefer it that way,' she told him. 'And I would also prefer it if you would use your own entrance to your dressing-room, and that the connecting door remained closed and locked at all times.'

'I see,' he said, without a trace of emotion in his voice or on his face. 'And what is everyone going to think when this comes to light? Servants talk, you know, and a locked door between master and mistress is exceptionally good gossip material.'

'They may think what they choose,' Camilla said

haughtily. 'How we conduct our marriage is our business, and no one else's. I am ready to go down to dinner now, Javier.'

She swept grandly from the room, her hand lightly on his proffered arm. What she had just done, had, she knew, cut off the one, slender chance of their coming together. It removed any hope that she might have cherished, but her pride was revived and she felt better for it. How she would feel in the darkness of the night, lying in bed and knowing that the door between them was firmly locked, was another matter.

It is better this way, she told herself grimly, or one night she might be unable to prevent herself from rushing into the dressing-room and throwing herself into his arms. Anula had won, she thought unhappily. Camilla had no more weapons with which to fight.

After this, Camilla spent as much time as she could out of doors riding, usually alone. The rains were expected soon, and when they came she knew they would make it virtually impossible to get out. The thought of being shut in, day after day, week after week, in the claustrophobic atmosphere of the house filled her with foreboding, and she made the most of what dry weather remained.

Often she found herself going back, drawn irresistibly to the ruined city, but she did not see the temple dancer again, and the memory of that night took on the quality of a dream which vanishes on waking, and then returns in snatches to haunt one throughout the day.

One morning, Camilla was disturbed by a strange cry, somewhere between a moan and a scream, which rang through the house. It came from the direction of Doña Lucia's room, and Camilla ran along the corridor to see what was troubling her mother-in-law, only to find a minor commotion taking place.

Doña Lucia was moaning unintelligibly, her eyes were vague and distraught. Lola had her arms round her mistress, trying in vain to comfort her, whilst Phillip hopped from one foot to the other, as if unsure what action to take.

'What's wrong?' Camilla demanded tersely.

'It's that half-crazed sister of mine,' he said crudely. 'She's run off with Piet van der Viert, of all people.'

Apparently, Helen had not been in her room when the maid took in her morning tea, which was unusual, but it was not until later that it was discovered that some of her clothes and personal possessions and all her jewels were missing.

'She left this,' Phillip concluded, handing Camilla a piece of white notepaper.

'I have gone away with Piet,' Helen had written simply. 'Please do not try to follow me, my mind is made up. Forgive me, but this is the only way.'

Lola helped Doña Lucia into her room, and they could still hear her hysterical sobbing from behind the closed door.

'We are going to look fools all over the island when it gets around that my sister has run off with our assistant manager,' Phillip said disgustedly.

Camilla regarded him with contempt.

'Is that the only thing that matters—that people will snigger at you behind your back?' she said. 'Doesn't it occur to you to think about your sister's happiness—to think that maybe this is what she wants?'

'Will it make her happy to run off with a fellow like that, without a penny beyond what he earns here, which will cease forthwith?' he retorted.

'I don't know the answer to that,' Camilla admitted. 'But Helen must have felt it was a chance she had to take.'

'Bah!' snorted Phillip. 'You women and your romantic nonsense! Someone should have told my sister that life is not like one of those sentimental books she reads! Just wait until Javier gets in. We'll ride after them and haul her back in no time, and boot that fellow clean off the island!'

As always in a crisis, word had been sent to Javier. He listened grimly to Phillip's rendition of what had happened, whilst Camilla stood nearby, taking in all that was said.

'I arranged to meet Piet in the fields this morning,' Javier said. 'I thought it was strange when he didn't turn up. I can't believe he persuaded Helen to go off with him, out of the blue. There must have been something going on between them for some time, without our knowledge.'

'There was,' Camilla said, and both men turned on her in amazement.

'You knew!' Phillip said accusingly. 'You knew, and you connived at this with her!'

'There's no call to speak to Camilla in that manner,' Javier said dangerously. 'I'll talk to *you* in private,' he told his wife, ushering her into the drawing-room and closing the door. 'Now, tell me everything you know about this.'

'It isn't a great deal.' She faced him courageously. 'I had no idea they were planning to elope, of that I can assure you. But yes, I knew there was something between them.'

'And you said nothing? A single girl, living under my protection, is having an affair with one of my employees, and you see fit to keep quiet about it? Isn't that a trifle irresponsible?'

Camilla flinched under the cold reprimand of his tone.

'I didn't see how I could divulge what I had found out by pure accident,' she defended herself. 'It would have been mean of me to do so. Who am I to begrudge anyone a little happiness?'

'Precisely,' came Javier's cutting retort. 'A *little* happiness is about all this escapade will bring either of them.'

'Helen was terrified of her mother finding out,' Camilla persisted. 'And if I had told her? You see what her reaction would have been.'

'Did it not occur to you that you might have told *me*?' he demanded.

'No,' Camilla said bluntly. 'I am sorry, Javier, but it did not. Our relationship is not such that I feel I can come to you with confidences.'

He gave a weary smile, and his anger appeared to evaporate all at once.

'No,' he said resignedly. 'I suppose it isn't. But you might have averted a good deal of heartbreak all around if you had told me. You see, what is not generally known at Ratnagalla, what Helen herself most probably did not know, is that, casting aside all question of the suitability of the match, Piet is not free to marry Helen. He has a wife in Amsterdam from whom he is separated, but who refuses to divorce him.'

Camilla gasped.

'Oh, poor Helen!' she exclaimed. 'What are we going to do?'

A shadow of a smile illumined the proud features.

'*I* am going to ride after my sister and try to persuade her of her own foolishness,' he said. 'Meanwhile, you are going to sit here at Ratnagalla and bite your nails, and reflect on the folly of keeping secrets from your husband.'

Looking up doubtfully at him, she saw that in spite of the seriousness of the situation, there was a rueful humour in his eyes.

'Oh, Camilla,' he said, 'this is a nest of snakes you've been flung into.'

Javier was away from Ratnagalla for several days, his longest absence from the estate since his father's death. Without him, and with no assistant manager to take over, Camilla did not see how the estate could function.

The pluckers and kanganies could continue to work in the fields, but without the close supervision of the *Periya Durai*, the estate was bound to suffer.

She came to this conclusion in the first hour after Javier had left, and decided that she could not simply sit around in this crisis, to which she had herself contributed, and let things go to pieces. She and Phillip would have to sink their differences and keep Ratnagalla functioning between them.

But when she approached him with a suggestion that he took over the field supervision, he shook his head morosely.

'It wouldn't work, Camilla, and it's not merely my natural inclination to idleness which makes me say that. Those labourers know I don't know a damn' thing about tea, the kanganies know much more about it than I do. They aren't going to respect any decision I make. I haven't even sufficient knowledge to make any decision. I don't know when to prune and when to let alone, can't tell red spider from copper blight, or how to treat either. I can ride around and try to look busy, but it wouldn't fool anyone.'

Camilla frowned. There was some truth in what he said, she could see, and she came to a quick decision.

'Well then, will you ride over to Hazelgrove with me, to see Mr Carstairs?' she asked.

Phillip shrugged.

'If you like, but Carstairs is a coffee man. I don't see how he can help us.'

'Maybe, but he told me he once worked on a tea estate, and he'll know enough to help us out for a short time—if he will,' she said.

Make what arrangements you think are necessary, Javier had told her before he left. His departure had inevitably been too rapid for him to leave explicit instructions, but he had left Ratnagalla in her hands, and she was doing the only thing she could think of. And so she and Phillip rode out shortly afterwards, hoping to reach Hazelgrove before nightfall.

'And no nonsense,' Camilla warned him, her eyes wary. She indicated her riding crop. 'If you so much as touch me, I shall use this. I mean it, Phillip.'

'You don't have to worry,' he assured her forcefully. 'I've learned my lesson with you, my dear Camilla, and I'd as soon make advances to an angry tigress. Besides, Javier would undoubtedly shoot me on his return, and no woman is worth it. But to change the subject, there is one thing you appear not to have thought of. You're planning to bring Carstairs back to Ratnagalla, but you've seen the state mother's in, and you know she hates strangers in the house.'

'I know, but it can't be helped,' Camilla said briskly. 'Doña Lucia will simply have to keep to her room— which she probably will be doing, anyhow, and we shall tell Mr Carstairs that she is indisposed—which is true.'

Phillip looked sharply at her.

'I think you know more about my mother's indisposition than you have any business knowing,' he said.

'I'm not a fool, Phillip,' she said curtly. 'And since I live in the same house, and I am married to your brother, it is as much my business as yours.'

It was late when they arrived at Hazelgrove, and the Carstairs were surprised and pleased to see them. Food was provided at once, and servants sent scurrying to prepare rooms for the unexpected guests.

Camilla explained quickly the purpose of her visit. Her husband had been obliged to leave on urgent family business, their assistant manager was also absent, and there was no one suitably qualified to look after the estate. If he were not too busy, would Mr Carstairs consider coming over to Ratnagalla for a few days, just to keep an eye on things?

Mr Carstairs was scarcely busy at all. He was waiting only for the sale of Hazelgrove to be completed, and then he and his wife would be packed and en route to their new life in the Malay states. He was flattered by Camilla's request, and only too glad to help her out.

'But it's years since I had anything to do with tea,' he demurred, 'and I've never coped with an estate the size of Ratnagalla.'

'It's only for a few days,' Camilla said pleadingly. 'I'm sure you know enough to keep things running smoothly until my husband returns.'

'Of course he does, and naturally we shall be pleased to help you,' his wife said decisively. 'You go with Mrs Ballantyne, Donald. I've plenty of packing and sorting out to keep me occupied here.'

So the next morning, very early, the three of them set out on the return journey, and the temporary manager of Ratnagalla, looking very pleased with herself, was ready to go out on his evening round of the fields. Camilla went with him, to explain briefly to the kanganies that Mr Carstairs would be in charge until the *Periya Durai* got back.

For the next few days she was so busy she scarcely had time to think. There was, as always, the house to run, although this she left largely in Lal's capable hands. Carstairs, she thought, had enough to do supervising the large and unfamiliar estate, so she went down to the factory and told Mac about the arrangements she had made, and the rest of the time she spent in the office, struggling with the accounts and the paperwork, setting aside what could wait until Javier's return, dealing with urgent letters which had to have a reply of some kind, and endeavouring to make sense of the book-keeping and bring it up to date.

She had never done anything like this in her life before, but she was aided by a quick mind which absorbed knowledge easily, and by her husband's clear and meticulous business methods, which meant that she found everything in order, and only had to follow the procedure laid down. The engineer and the factory workers soon became accustomed to seeing Mrs Ballantyne's trim figure in their midst as she made her way to the office, and her smooth fair head visible through the small window, bent over the accounts. Mac saw to it that she was well supplied with pots of tea at regular intervals, and from time to time would pop his head round the door to see how she was getting on, and assure her that she was 'a grand lass'.

By the time she made her way back to the house for a welcome bath and change of clothes in readiness for dinner, Camilla was hot and exhausted. But she was aware of an immense inner satisfaction, a feeling of having put all of her abilities and her energy to a worthwhile purpose. So this was the hard, stimulating world the men lived in, whilst their women occupied themselves with menus and flower-arranging, and telling servants what to do. She wondered if the day would ever come when women would march into this world under their own colours.

'Here comes the busy planter, back from a day's toil,' Phillip said, as Camilla joined him and Carstairs for dinner. 'I'll swear, if she could supervise the field work herself, she would do it, and we wouldn't need you, old man.'

There was mockery in his voice, but a touch of jealousy also, as if Camilla's competence and willingness to take over gave him cause for shame.

'I think she's a marvel,' Donald Carstairs said warmly. 'Mr Ballantyne will have every reason to be proud of her when he gets back.'

Javier arrived back at Ratnagalla one afternoon, after an absence of about a week. Camilla was in the office, and so knew nothing of his arrival until he came and found her there.

Even then, she did not look up as the door opened, expecting it to be a bearer with a tea tray.

'Just put it down on the small table, I'll help myself in a moment,' she said, frowning abstractedly and chewing the end of her pen.

'I'll pour, if you wish,' said her husband's voice, and Camilla dropped the pen and looked up, startled, to see him setting down the tray on the desk before her. 'This was just on its way, so I thought I would surprise you.'

'You certainly did that,' she said, smiling. 'It's all right—I'll pour.'

He sat down facing her, his expression puzzled and pleased at the same time.

'No more than I was surprised to find *you* in here,' he said. 'And you brought Carstairs over from Hazelgrove, I hear. Good thinking, Camilla. I see I needn't have worried about the estate whilst I've been away. With you in charge, everything is running most efficiently.'

She blushed with pleasure at his unstinted praise.

'I could not simply sit back and do nothing,' she said. 'But tell me—what happened? Did you find Helen?'

He shook his head.

'No. They were always one step ahead of us. They must have left during the night, whilst we were asleep, and were on the train from Nuwara Eliya to Colombo before we even knew they were gone. I made enquiries in Colombo, but they had taken ship as soon as they arrived, bound for Java. I believe there's a considerable Dutch colony there, and van der Viert may have contacts.'

'So what did you do?'

He shrugged. 'I wasn't prepared to follow my errant sister to Java. I wrote a letter addressed to her, care of the shipping line, explaining to her she could not marry Piet, and telling her that she was welcome to come home again if she wished. I told her . . .' he paused, 'I told her other things, too, which I thought she should know.'

He did not expand on this any further, leaving Camilla to wonder vaguely what those 'other things' were. Whatever they were, her woman's instinct told her that it would make no difference. Helen Ballantyne had escaped from a sterile existence, and even though she was now in a perilous situation, with a lover who could not marry her, cut off from the comforts of her wealthy background, Camilla knew she would never come back to Ratnagalla.

She said, 'Have you told your mother?'

'Yes. Someone had to, and I felt it would come best from me. She's in her room with the blinds drawn, and Lola waving sal volatile under her nose. I haven't told her, or anyone else, that Piet van der Viert is already married. I thought that would be too much for her to take. She would prefer to think of Helen married, if unsuitably, than living in sin.'

He drained his teacup and got to his feet.

'Are you ready to come up to the house? I think I shall change and accompany Carstairs on the evening rounds,' he said, an impatient eagerness in his voice. 'My God, I've missed Ratnagalla!'

And I have missed you, Camilla thought sadly. Even while she had run his house, and his office, with scarcely a minute to draw breath, she had missed him, deep inside herself, where her innermost emotions lived. But she could never tell him that.

Together they walked up to the house, through the gardens bathed in the afternoon sun. The following morning Donald Carstairs rode back to Hazelgrove, accompanied by much gratitude and good wishes, and Javier resumed his role of *Periya Durai*.

'I shall have to start making enquiries, casting around for a new assistant,' he said to Camilla, who had risen early to have breakfast with him on his first day back at work.

'Do you need one? There's me,' she said, only half jesting.

'Admirable though you are, you cannot ride round the

fields, supervising the pluckers and making decisions about planting, pruning, and so forth,' he pointed out.

'No, but I can do office work,' she said eagerly. 'All right, so I'm not so efficient as you are, and it takes me longer, but I can learn—*am* learning. Why not?'

'Your ability is not in question,' he said. 'You did an excellent job, and I am grateful to you, but that was for a short time only, in an emergency. You cannot seriously suggest that you become a full-time clerk and book-keeper.'

'I don't see why not,' Camilla said mutinously. 'Lal takes care of the house, and anything I do in that province has to be done by stealth since your mother resents it. I am not really your wife, I do not have children to take care of, nor am I likely to. I must do something, Javier.'

He stood up, abruptly, his patience running out, a frown lining his forehead.

'Camilla, I don't have time to argue with you about this.'

'No, because you know it's the truth, and you would rather avoid it,' she flung at him, angrily. For a moment, they glared furiously at each other, and then without another word he turned and strode off down the path.

Camilla stared miserably at her untouched breakfast, which she now had no desire to finish. Once again, they were at one another's throats, after so short a time when she had basked in his approval and esteem. Now it was all gone, they were back exactly where they were before, simply because, once again, she had reminded him of her ambiguous and unsatisfactory position in his household.

CHAPTER
SEVEN

THAT night, the splendour of the sunset was marred by dark, heavy clouds piling up behind the mountains, and during the night Camilla awoke to hear rain beating against her window, heavy and persistent. The monsoon had come, sweeping in from the Indian ocean with long-pent ferocity.

In the morning it was still raining, and a heavy mist cloaked the atmosphere, cutting off the hills from view. The temperature had dropped several degrees, and Camilla was glad of her warmer clothes. The gardens were drenched, water dripped from the eaves, and their every activity was carried on to the sound of the rain falling constantly.

And so it went on, day after day. Sometimes the mist lifted and the rain eased to a persistent drizzle, sometimes it increased in intensity, bucketing down from the sky in long, straight ribbons. Sometimes a howling wind got up behind it, driving it around the house in whirling eddies of spray.

Only the very worst of the weather kept the pluckers from their work. Sacking aprons round their waists, and thick blankets known as 'cumblies' over their bent heads, they still moved industriously along the terraces, and whenever it was fit for them to be at work, Javier was out, too, driving himself unsparingly.

'If you are really serious about wanting to help,' he told Camilla, 'then you may do an hour or two in the office during the afternoons. We shall have to manage without an assistant, at least until the monsoon is over.'

'I shall be glad to do it,' she told him, and he gave a faint smile.

'I know you will, but it has to be understood and accepted that this is a temporary measure only.'

'Oh, very well,' she capitulated, telling herself that she would learn so much about the business of running a tea estate that when the time came he would not want to replace her.

Uncannily, he seemed to have divined her thoughts.

'I mean exactly what I say,' he warned her. 'You have a great talent for agreeing to something when it suits you in the hope of changing it when it no longer does. I can't be manipulated like that, Camilla.'

'Who should know that better than I?' she retorted, almost jauntily.

Doña Lucia, who had recovered sufficiently from the shock of Helen's defection to take her place amongst the family once more, found the mere idea of her daughter-in-law's work in the office unthinkable.

'It is degrading for a woman of quality to take such duties upon herself,' she said, with acid disapproval. 'Furthermore, it is quite unnecessary. Javier could manage—he always has done so before.'

'But if I can ease the burden, it makes sense for me to do so,' Camilla pointed out gently. 'I don't mind, in fact, I rather enjoy it.'

'That,' Doña Lucia said frostily, 'is beside the point. It is not seemly. It is not your place. You are here in order to give my son a child, to carry on the da Silva line, and *that* is what you should be doing.'

Camilla would have loved nothing better, but she could not tell this proud, nervous woman that her son never visited his wife's bed, that they slept with a locked door between them, so with a sigh she relinquished the argument.

The days fell into a routine as regular as the falling rain, and with every one that passed, Camilla became increasingly knowledgeable and adept. Her double-entry book-keeping was almost as faultless as her husband's, she learned the purpose of all the different documents required in connection with the transportation and export of tea, and how to deal with them. From poring over books in the office in every spare minute she could snatch, she even learned the history of this fascinating plant, from its Chinese origins, via its sojourn in Assam, to its arrival in Ceylon.

'The botanical name of the tea bush is *Camellia sinensis*,' she told her husband delightedly one afternoon, when he called in the office to explain some details of the accounts which were puzzling her. 'Of course, you would know that, wouldn't you, but it seems so appropriate, since my name is also derived from the flower, camellia.'

'Almost as if your unfortunate parents decided at your birth that you were destined to be a planter's wife, and gave you a name which would be fitting,' he said, but the light of mockery in his eyes was not cruel. 'Is that what you are suggesting?'

'No, of course not!' she said. 'My mother died when I was born, and so did not have the opportunity to consider my future. I was named for the flower that she loved, which was growing in her conservatory at the time, or so I am told. It is simply that I was reading this book, and the coincidence struck me.'

'I thought that perhaps living in Ceylon was giving you the eastern habit of seeing signs and portents in everything,' he said. 'A dangerous habit, since if anyone looks hard enough they can always find what they want to see, believe what it suits them to believe. Don't do that, Camilla. It would be a mistake.'

There could be no doubting that this was a warning he was giving her, and Camilla felt cold fingers of ice spreading out around her heart.

'You don't believe in destiny, then?' she asked lightly,

trying to ward off a growing sense of foreboding.

He leaned against a filing cabinet, and regarded her with eyes which were both sober and appraising. Camilla had changed since Helen's unexpected flight had given her the opportunity to have a hand in the management of Ratnagalla. She had matured, acquired a new confidence, a bloom which came from doing well something which she had never expected to do at all. In a sense, she was no longer a green girl, and this made what he had to say harder, and at the same time, more essential.

'I don't believe that the hand of destiny brought you and I together,' he said bluntly. 'Nor does it have to keep us that way, unless we both wish it.'

The cold fingers clutched harder, squeezing the breath out of her.

'But we are married,' she protested. 'Those whom God hath joined together . . .'

'A marriage which has not been consummated may be anulled,' he replied levelly, not taking his eyes from her face.

'You want me to go,' Camilla said dully. 'You want to send me back to England, like an article bought from a shop which has turned out to be unsuitable.'

'No. Like a real person, someone of worth, who has a right to a life of her own.' Javier's eyes, and his voice, were steady, but Camilla's hands had begun to tremble and she clasped them firmly together.

'I have a life—here,' she said stubbornly.

'You have half a life,' he corrected her. 'You told me as much yourself, once. Remember?'

'But that was months ago!' Camilla objected. 'I have accepted that, now.'

'Have you?' he probed insistently, and Camilla was obliged to look down at the desk top. 'Can you say honestly, in your heart, that you have?'

She could not look into his eyes and answer that with a blatant lie, and she knew that if she did, he was too astute to believe her. Instead, she launched a desperate counter-attack.

'Is that all the thanks I get for managing Ratnagalla in your absence, for all the work and effort I have undertaken on your behalf? "Thank you very much, Camilla, but you may go home now, I shall not require you any more!"'

He said, 'You have been invaluable here these last weeks, and I am the first to admit it. That is precisely why I said what I did. I've wronged you, Camilla, deeply and unforgiveably, and it seems I have only just realised how much. Before, when you were just a girl I hardly knew, I was able to convince myself that it did not matter, that I could make you fit in with what I wanted to do. My mother would be content, life at Ratnagalla would settle down, I could get on with my work, and your feelings did not really enter into it.'

He paused, leaned forward with both hands resting on the desk, and looked deeply into the eyes she at last raised to his.

'Seeing you as you are now, I can no longer take that cavalier attitude towards you,' he told her. 'You are a woman who would be an asset to any man, and you deserve a real marriage, with children of your own. I can't hold you here, Camilla. I have too much respect for you.'

Her eyes blazed with pain and unshed tears.

'I don't want your respect!' she cried. 'I want your love!'

'That I am not free to give you,' he said.

Between them, a strange silence fell, and lengthened, tinged with sadness on both sides. Camilla sat as if turned to marble, but it was she who finally spoke.

A few short months ago, she would have been unable to contain so much hurt. She would have jumped up and rushed past him in tears. Now, her calm regained, she simply said, in a small, restrained voice, 'Would you excuse me? I should like to complete today's entries in the ledger before I go up to the house.'

'Of course,' he said politely, and made his exit as requested.

Camilla entered the figures in the ledger, forcing herself to concentrate on their accuracy and not on the scene which had just taken place. Only when the last column was complete, the ink dry, and the book back in its drawer, did she allow herself to go over it all in her mind.

She supposed that he had been honest with her. He had admitted at last the validity of her needs, and from there it was only a short step to setting her free so that she might find someone who could fulfill them. Honest, too, had been his uncompromising admission that he could not love her. I am not *free* to love you, he had said. No, because there was Anula, to whom he had already given his heart. He could not marry her and bring her to Ratnagalla as its mistress, such a thing would have created a scandal fit to kill his mother and set all Ceylon talking, but perhaps, in all but name, he felt himself married to her, and had vowed to be faithful to her. For that, Camilla could not find it in herself to blame him.

She tidied up the desk, locked the office, and made her way through the factory, remembering to wave and smile at Mac, who, as usual, was half in and half out of one of his precious machines. Slowly, she walked up the path, indifferent to the rain which had slowed to a thin, drizzle, through which a watery sun was trying to break. Out on the hills, the pluckers moved endlessly, she heard snatches of melodious Tamil as they called to one another. In the gardens, the roses drooped miserably, their petals dashed by the power of the rain, but they would bloom again in September, when the monsoon tracked away from Ceylon, and the sun returned in its full glory to the resplendent land.

But would she see it? Would she wake again to the sun

streaming through her windows, the crisp, fragrant air? Would she ride through the lush, verdant hills, and see the pluckers returning from the fields at evening, the heavy cane baskets on their backs, full of freshly-picked leaf to be weighed? Would she watch from the verandah as the sun died magnificently behind the peaks, streaking the sky with vibrant colour?

No, and neither would she see Javier striding up the path in his well-worn jacket and battered hat, she would not see his proud, dark face opposite her at the dinner table, not his tall frame relaxed in one of the cane chairs, a glass held between his long, capable fingers. She would not hear his rich, resonant voice, as quick to praise as to reprimand, softening as he spoke of his deep love for the land which was his.

He would send her away because his stern conscience had already decided that in keeping her here, tied to him and yet not really married, he had wronged her. Nothing she could say or do would change that decision, she knew his implacable mind too well. He would send her away, and Ratnagalla would be just a memory.

But do not think, Camilla said inwardly, *never* think that I will stop loving you, for over that you have no power, and nor have I.

The brief respite from the monsoon proved all too short, for that night it began to rain with greater force than it had before. In the morning, the whole world was transformed into a watery gouache, in which all colours merged into an indeterminate greyness. Nothing was visible beyond the streaming curtain of rain, hills, sky, even the lower reaches of the garden had dissolved into nothingness.

There was no work done in the fields that day, or for several days thereafter, the terraces would be too wet for the pluckers to stand upright. Nor did any of the tea, packed and ready, leave for the rail-head at Nuwara

Eliya, since the route was impassable, even for the mules which were used for this transport. For Ratnagalla, the outside world had temporarily ceased to exist, there was no way in or out.

'How long will it go on like this?' Camilla, asked, standing at the window and watching the rain sheeting down.

Phillip shrugged.

'It's difficult to say. Every year during the monsoon we are cut off for a time, could be a few days, or even a few weeks,' he said. 'Wretched business, isn't it? Its so boring when one can't even go out and shoot something to relieve the monotony.'

Camilla could not really share his frustration. For her, the apalling weather, which made it impossible for anyone to get into or out of Ratnagalla, was not unwelcome, in fact it was a blessing. For while the rains continued with such ferocity there could be no more talk of her leaving.

She knew that this only postponed the event she faced with so much dread, but every day she remained here was, to her, a gift from heaven, another day which kept her from the heartbreak, the loneliness that lay ahead.

It would come, she knew. Javier would not have spoken in such a way unless he fully intended carrying out his plan. She had no idea what formalities had to be undergone to bring about the anulment of a marriage, but she had already decided that she would not sit around and wait for it to happen. She refused to hang on until the last humiliating minute, her pride had taken too much of a battering already, and she would leave with as much dignity as she was able to salvage.

The moment he came to her and said, quite definitely and beyond all possibility of misunderstanding, 'Camilla, our marriage is over, I want you to go,' her bags would be packed and she would go, without a word, without a tear, and, she promised herself, without re-proach.

And so she was grateful for the rains which, for the moment at least, took the awful decision out of their hands. A few days—a few weeks, Phillip had said. Either way, so short a time. Camilla looked out at the streaming heavens each morning and breathed a sigh of relief.

Ratnagalla had been isolated from the world for several days when, one morning, one of the kanganies came to the house, urgently requesting to see the *Periya Durai*. This in itself was unusual, and the house servant, who considered himself superior to those who worked in the fields, sniffed and left the man standing out on the rain-dashed verandah whilst he went to fetch the master.

The conversation was brief. Javier put on his jacket and went off with the man without hesitation.

'I wonder what all that was about,' Camilla said curiously.

'Oh, some dispute in the lines, I expect,' Phillip said carelessly. 'When they've nothing much to do, fights and arguments can break out easily. Usually, they don't amount to much, but occasionally, one fellow might take it into his head to stick a knife in his neighbour. All part of the rich pattern of estate life.' He grinned at his sister-in-law's concerned expression. 'Don't worry. Javier will sort it out.'

But when her husband returned, Camilla could see that her concern had not been misplaced. There was more amiss than a quarrel amongst unoccupied workers.

'There's sickness in the lines,' he told them briefly. 'A couple of them are down with fever, vomiting and abdominal pains. I've isolated them in the hospital shed, and we can only hope it's a lone incident, or that we've caught it in time to stop its spreading.'

Camilla said, 'You don't sound very hopeful. What do you think it is?'

He regarded her with the utmost gravity.

'I think it's cholera,' he said.

Phillip blanched.

'My God!' he exclaimed. 'That could spread through the lines like a forest fire! And we can't even send for help!'

Javier said, 'Then you had better pray that I am wrong. We should know by tomorrow, one way or the other.'

For the remainder of the day, the house hung suspended in a pall of fear. Everyone went about their normal business, meals were served, duties done, but there was a hushed anxiety in the air. In the evening, Javier went down to the Tamil quarters and reported no change in the condition of the two men so far affected and no further incidence of the symptoms.

'I've read everyone the usual lecture about all water and milk having to be boiled, and the windows of the hospital shed are fly-screened to prevent insects carrying the disease,' he said. 'There's nothing more we can do tonight.'

By morning, there were three more cases, and the two men who had been taken ill the previous day were now experiencing the severe muscle cramps which accompanied loss of fluid from the body.

Camilla took one look at Javier's face and said, 'It *is* cholera, isn't it?'

'I'm sure of it, now,' he said. 'Have you seen cholera before, Camilla?'

She nodded.

'There was an outbreak in Calcutta, when I was a child. My ayah died of it. I think I ran a temperature for a few days, and they were all very worried, but I recovered, and my grandmother said it might have given me some resistance to it.'

He said, 'That's good, because I am going to need all

the help I can get. You know what I'm talking about, I presume?'

'Of course. These people are going to require nursing,' she said steadily. 'I'll help, in any way I can.'

'Be quite sure of what you are committing yourself to, before you start,' he warned her. 'This is a killer, it's highly contagious, and no respecter of persons. It's also unpleasant to a high degree, with vomiting and diarrhoea. Looking after cholera sufferers is not for the squeamish.'

'I know that. I've said I'll help, and I will. And there's someone else who will, too—Mohini.'

'Mohini—in the lines, amongst her social inferiors?' he said incredulously. 'Are you sure?'

'Quite sure. Because these are sick people, and deserving of her pity. She's calm and capable, she was as good as a rock when Fanny was ill. I'll fetch her.'

As Camilla had predicted, the Indian girl did not hesitate. She helped Camilla change into the plainest, unfussiest gown she owned, then both women set out with Javier to the Tamil quarters.

The hospital shed was a plain, clean, spartan building to the rear of the lines, furnished only with rows of beds. It was scarcely used. For minor ailments the labourers preferred to remain in their own quarters with their families; only in the case of highly infectious diseases would they submit to being isolated from the community. And they had never had cholera at Ratnagalla, Javier told Camilla, although he had seen it on other estates. The advantages of being remote, which helped prevent infection reaching them, turned against them when it finally did, making it impossible to send for help.

However, Camilla knew, as did Javier, that with this disease, there was little the most skilled doctor could do. Once the infection had struck they could only try to contain it, for there was no known and certain cure.

Isolation of the patients was the first requirement, but

this broke down as the first child was admitted, and they realised the impossibility of barring the sobbing mother from the premises.

'We shall have to let the mothers stay with their sick children,' Camilla urged. 'We can't shut them out—it's too cruel, and they will only stand outside the windows, crying and disturbing those who are inside.'

'Very well,' said Javier, 'mothers of sick children may stay, but once in, they observe the quarantine. They can't go back and forth to their families, spreading the infection. I suppose they might as well help with the nursing. There's going to be too much for the three of us to do.'

Soberly taking note of the rapidly filling beds, Camilla realised that he was right. Their outbreak was fast reaching epidemic proportions.

Throughout the day they were kept busy, cleaning both patients and beds, swilling floors with hot water, administering drinks of carefully measured boiled water to try and prevent dehydration, and simply comforting those for whom they could do no more. At first, the stench was unbearable, but as time passed, Camilla found that she began to accept it as an unchangeable fact of life, and when she stepped outside for a few moments respite, the damp air hit her like a hammer with its clean sweetness, and she gulped it down thirstily.

Half way through the long afternoon, the door opened and Doña Lucia appeared. Setting down a huge bottle she had carried under one arm, she shook out her dripping umbrella and snapped it shut.

'Go and attend to your business, my son,' she said. 'I shall take your place here.'

'I have no business at the moment, mother, apart from this,' he replied.

'What nonsense!' said Doña Lucia. 'Your factory is still working, is it not? Don't you have things to attend to there?'

'Yes, the factory is working, although for how long, I don't know,' Javier said wearily. 'And yes, there are things I should be doing. But I'm not sure you ought to be here, mother. You haven't been well yourself, lately.'

'This is the estate your father built up, and these are his people,' his mother said calmly, drawing herself up. 'If I am not well enough to be here when I am needed, then it is time I was . . . elsewhere.'

Javier smiled. 'Very well, mother, if you insist. I shall go and do what has to be done in the factory and office.' He looked round at them all. 'First of all, I shall go up to the house, bathe and have a complete change of clothes, and I'm sure I don't need to remind any of you to do the same when you come out from this building. We must observe the strictest hygiene if we are going to avoid coming down with this thing ourselves.'

When he had gone, Doña Lucia looked up and down the row of patients with the practised eye and stoic demeanour of a woman whose whole life had been spent in the tropics. The hysterical woman whose nerves gave way at the slightest impact of reality, who passed much of her time in a darkened bedroom, had vanished, for the present, and in her place was a proud and resourceful matriarch. She picked up the bottle she had brought with her.

'This is some cholera mixture Dr Davies once gave me, in case we should ever need it,' she said. 'It's a solution of certain salts and chemicals, he said, needed to replace those lost by the body. We only have this bottle, so don't waste it on those who are already too far gone—such as that unfortunate man in the corner.'

The two young women followed her gaze to where the first cholera case lay. He was scarcely breathing, his pulse low, his hands and feet already blue with cold. Mohini tenderly put a blanket over him, her huge eyes brimming with sorrow.

'No use crying, my girl,' Doña Lucia said testily.

'You'll see plenty more like that before this is over. Now—help me get this inside the ones we may be able to save.'

Doling out the medicine, Camilla had little time to reflect on the amazing transformation in her mother-in-law, but as they worked steadily, together, maid, mistress and young bride, all differences set aside in the mutual endeavour, she had a glimpse of the woman Doña Lucia might have been, free from the awful malaise which was eating her away from within. And she had cause to be glad that Doña Lucia's strength had rallied at this time, when it was so badly needed.

Even Phillip deigned to put in an appearance, hovering sheepishly outside the hospital shed in the pouring rain. He looked so out of place, his clothing drenched, his normally sleek hair plastered to his head, that Camilla took pity on him and went to the door to see what he wanted.

'Phillip, you're soaked to the skin,' she expostulated. 'For goodness sake, come in out of the wet!'

He stood just inside the doorway.

'I can't come in there, I just can't,' he said pleadingly. 'It isn't that I'm so afraid of catching the damn thing, I simply can't stand the smell of carbolic, and . . . and all the other smells . . . nor the sight of those poor wretches sweating it out. But if there's anything else I can do to help . . .'

A smile lit Camilla's tired face.

'I understand,' she said, and in a way, she did. There were people who just could not abide being around sickness, people whom the sight of pain and suffering in others reduced to gibbering wrecks. Such people were more hindrance than help in a situation like this, and she did not think anything would be gained by insisting that Phillip come in and do his share with the sick and dying. It was, anyway, not considered man's work, and the fact that her husband had undertaken it was another indication of his exceptional quality. She accepted Phillip's inhibitions, and set him to work organising yet more hot water, taking messages to Lal for tea to be provided, and so on.

After all, she reasoned, he·was equally at risk as the rest of them, he could quite easily catch cholera from contact with them. Anyone of us, she told herself, could be incubating the killer disease, and she was surprised how little the thought worried her.

Was it because she did not care very much what happened to her, after she was no longer married to Javier? It was a curiously liberating discovery. Here she was, tending people who were desperately ill, some of whom were near death, and would die in spite of all their efforts, and she had no fear of being infected by them, because it simply did not matter.

Camilla turned and went back to her patients, her face was calm, smiling and beautiful, as if she had just seen a vision. If she had worked hard before, from that moment she gave herself unstintingly to their care. No task was too hard, too menial, or too revolting for her to undertake, she held bowls beneath the heads of retching men and women, stripped and replaced excreta-soaked bedding, all with the same quiet, beatific patience. She was all theirs, holding nothing in reserve, because for her there was nothing for which to withhold herself.

And it was she who witnessed the death of the man who had been the first to report sick, and who sat at his bedside as he died. The day before yesterday, this inert body had been a young, strong, healthy man in the prime of life, accustomed to hard physical work, and she recalled once more the words which had come to her when Fanny died, so long ago, it now seemed . . . that death, the grave and forgetfulness may be the work of two days . . . only this time, the cunning hunter was out in the open, his claws unsheathed, he was not content to stalk in the shadows and pick off the unwary. Another man, and then a child, died in quick, almost indecent succession.

The sound of his voice outside alerted her to Javier's return.

'All this soiled bedding will have to be removed and burned,' he was telling Phillip.

'Burned? In this rain? How the devil—'

'Get some labourers to construct a shelter and burn it bit by bit, under cover,' Javier suggested patiently. 'The rain will prevent the shelter from catching fire.'

Inside the hospital shed, his eyes flickered over the three tired women.

'If we are to keep going, we must fit in periods of rest,' he pointed out. 'And I am not being callous and advocating neglect of the sick. It is a necessity.'

'Then you should speak first to your wife,' Doña Lucia said. 'She is pushing herself harder than anyone.'

'Camilla?' Javier said questioningly. 'Enough. Go up to the house and lie down for an hour, have some food.'

She shook her head.

'How could anyone feel like eating?' she protested. 'I'm all right as I am, I assure you.'

For answer, he took her very firmly by the arm and steered her outside, ignoring her objections. The rain streamed relentlessly down, and unexpectedly, he swung her up into his arms and ran with her through the lines and up through the gardens to the house, while the rain soaked them both, sticking their clothes together and spreading loose strands of her wet hair on his shoulder. For Camilla, tired and spent as she was, it was a moment out of time when she savoured his closeness, and too soon he was setting her on her feet in the hall.

She had not thought she was so exhausted until she paused from her labours, it did not strike her just how much effort, mental and physical, she had expended. Bathed, scrubbed and changed into clean clothes, she lay down on the bed, intending only to close her eyes for a few minutes, and was asleep instantly.

She awoke with a guilty start, struggling through layers of drowsiness, aware that she should not be here, there was something else she should be attending to . . . if she could only remember what it was. Then it came back to her, and she sat up hastily, trying to collect her scattered senses together.

'Are you awake, Camilla?' Javier tapped on the door and came into the bedroom.

'Oh yes . . . someone should have woken me before, I never meant to sleep so long.'

'You haven't,' he said. 'It's only dinner time.'

Although she was still protesting that she did not want anything to eat, indeed, could not face food, he shepherded her down to the dining-room and poured whisky generously into two glasses.

'I know it isn't considered a ladies' drink, but it will revive you and warm you up,' he said. 'Used moderately, it will also alleviate a little of the horror.'

Camilla forced herself to drink, and let the fiery liquid trickle down her throat. She coughed a little, and he patted her on the back. 'Not so quickly,' he warned. 'The objective is to restore your vitality, not to choke yourself. You have done the work of several women today, Camilla.'

'So have Mohini and your mother,' she replied quickly.

'I know, but you seem bent on driving yourself harder than anyone else. Why?' he asked, not unkindly, and she lifted clear hazel eyes to meet his, unflinching.

'Because *they* need me,' she said simply. She could have said, because all the love I have for you, which you refuse to accept, cannot be wasted, thrown away on the air, dissipated in tears and accusations. It has to be channelled somewhere, put to some useful purpose, and I have found the answer.

Moments later, when Lal's delicious soup was placed

in front of her fragrant and enticing, she turned her head away, unable to bear the thought. In spite of all her vigorous scrubbing in the bath, the sour atmosphere of the sick room still lingered in her nostrils, the memory of all the suffering she had witnessed came between her and her usually healthy appetite.

'I can't,' she said.

'Oh, but you can,' Javier said gently, but expecting obedience. 'You can and you must, even if you have to force down every mouthful. Otherwise you simply will not have the energy to do what has to be done. What's more, your weakness will lower your resistance. Now, come on . . . try just a little. It's good. You know Lal will be mortally offended if his soup goes back to the kitchen untouched. He might even leave us, and then what should we do?'

In this half-jocular manner, he cajoled, encouraged and bullied her into swallowing a few mouthfuls of whatever was put in front of them. Realising the sense of his argument, Camilla did try, although to eat at all demanded a conscious effort to suppress the mind and concentrate only on the demands of her body. She did not fail to notice that Javier, too, ate only sparingly.

'I must get back down there and see what is happening,' she fretted as the plates were cleared away. 'Mohini has worked her fingers to the bone, and your mother has been simply marvellous.'

'Yes,' he said, frowning, 'but I wonder how long she can go on, before she cracks beneath the strain?'

He must have spent much of his young manhood trying to protect his mother from anything which would cause her distress, Camilla realised. That was one of the principal reasons for their marriage. Doña Lucia was anxious for him to bring a bride to Ratnagalla, and he had complied, to alleviate her anxiety. But did he not also realise that his mother expected him to provide an heir, to continue the ancient lineage of which she was so proud? Camilla sighed heavily, and looked up to find his eyes fixed compassionately on her face.

'It has hardly been a happy time for you at Ratnagalla,' he observed. 'My sister showed you little friendship, my brother attempted to seduce you, and with my mother, you never know where you are. Your maid died suddenly, to make things worse. And I myself have not lived up to your expectations.'

She hesitated before replying. All that he had said was true, but still, there had been moments of unforgettable beauty which had given her a kind of happiness. Riding with Javier along the tea terraces, the day he had shown her round the estate, and coming back from Hazelgrove through the bright, mysterious moonlight. There had been that oddly ecstatic experience in the ruined city, and a different, more painful ecstasy, those few moments when he had forgotten himself, and held her fiercely in his arms. And Ratnagalla itself had never disappointed her, she had loved it from the first, the lush sunsets and crisp mornings, the bright green hills and the jagged peaks beyond. It would stay with her always, no matter where she went or what happened to her.

She said, 'It would be wrong to say that I have no regrets, but my regrets are not for anything that has happened, only for what might have been. I do not blame your family for their treatment of me, each of them is a victim of his or her own circumstances. Your mother is a sick woman. Helen was just a frustrated girl, and Phillip is kicking futilely against a fate he thinks has dealt him all the wrong cards.'

He waited as a servant brought in coffee and set it in front of them, and when they were alone again, he said, with a touch of irony, 'You are uncommonly generous. Does your magnanimity extend to me?'

'Yes,' she replied promptly, with a calm and sedate composure. 'I have no bitterness against you, Javier— not any more. You cannot help loving Anula, and I accept your need to be free of me.'

He pushed aside his coffee cup so fiercely that Camilla feared for the delicate china.

'My need is for *you* to be free!' he said explosively. 'Can't you see that?'

'No, Javier, I can't,' she said levelly. 'It is you, not I, who love someone else.'

He stood up abruptly, walked to the window and gazed out at the streaming wetness beyond the glass. Then he turned and came back to the table, but did not resume his seat. Instead, he stood looking down at her, his face unreadable.

'It is time you knew the truth,' he said. 'That much I owe you. Anula is not the reason why you and I can never be truly man and wife, why you must leave Ratnagalla. God help me, I never loved Anula!'

Camilla lifted puzzled, uncomprehending eyes to his.

'But she is your mistress?' she said questioningly.

He inclined his head.

'To begin with, she was my father's mistress,' he said. 'Long ago, so he told me, when they were first married, my father had an affair with another woman. It upset my mother so badly he vowed it would never happen again, and it never did, until she came. He was always restless, and she was incredibly beautiful, I suppose the temptation overcame him. She had her claws into him, thinking she had found a rich provider. People gossip, and my mother began to suspect. It was . . . breaking her up, so I pretended that I was the one who was keeping Anula.'

Camilla found she had been holding her breath. Now, she said, 'You must have been very convincing, for she believes it still, and so does Phillip. So did I.'

He gave a brief shrug.

'By that time, it was no longer a pretence,' he said quietly. 'After my father died, I became Anula's lover for a while. Perhaps I had pretended for so long that it spilled over into reality. No—I should not excuse myself with such facility. She was beautiful, in a dark, sensuous, atavistic way, and I am no better than any other man, if the truth were known. She offered herself, and I took her. But it was no more than a brief, unreasoning lust. I never loved her. I sent her away months ago, before your arrival.'

The thoughts jostled one another so hard in Camilla's mind it was difficult to seperate them and make sense of what he was saying.

'You sent her away? But she is here. I have seen her,' she said.

'Where? When?' he interrogated sharply. 'I heard she was now the mistress of a Sinhalese businessman in Colombo.'

Camilla had no choice but to tell him of her midnight excursion to the ruined city, where she had seen Anula dancing. He listened gravely, seeming more concerned at the thought of her riding about alone at night than by the news of the Tamil girl's reappearance in the district.

'That was a foolish and dangerous thing to do,' he reprimanded her, sternly.

But Camilla only shrugged away his concern.

'I came to no harm,' she said. 'I hardly thought it mattered to you, anyway.'

'What a childish and ridiculous remark!' he flared at her with sudden anger. 'Do you really believe that because I refused to share your bed I did not care for your safety, that I would view such foolhardy escapades with equanimity?'

'How do I know what I should believe?' she countered desperately. 'You took this Tamil girl as your mistress with the utmost ease, although you say you never loved her. But you steadfastly refused the love I was ready to give you. Why? Because I am less desirable than she, and you find me all too easy to resist?'

He laid a hand over hers on the table, to still her agitation.

'A woman like that, who goes from man to man as she pleases, is well able to take care of herself, and need not trouble any man's conscience,' he said, patiently and with great deliberation. 'But you came here as a young and innocent girl, Camilla, and it would have been no kindness in me to expose you to the risk of being my wife, in the fullest sense of the word.'

'Risk? What risk?' she demanded, now thoroughly confused and distressed.

'The dark threat which has shadowed the da Silvas for many generations,' he replied sombrely. 'Madness, Camilla. I am not talking simply of a certain nervousness and a tendency to hysteria, such as you see in my mother. That is merely one of its earlier stages. What I am referring to is raving insanity. It has touched one member of every generation of my mother's family for two hundred years. My grandmother finished up confined in an asylum somewhere in Europe. My mother knows, too, that sooner or later, this will be her fate, too, it is coming closer, inexorably, as the years pass.'

With a swift, dismissive gesture of the hand, he forestalled her protests.

'I may be spared. The instability was noticeable in Helen from an early age, which is why my mother was so against her marrying at all. But I am not prepared to give you a child who might inherit this terrible and incurable condition.'

Camilla sat for a long time looking down at the polished table top.

'Your father took the risk,' she whispered.

'Ah, yes. It was in his nature to take risks, and he needed the money, don't you see? He was allowed to marry the da Silva heiress because no one else dared to. This thing had been hushed up for so long, but rumours had begun to circulate. My mother, too, believes it is worth taking the risk, for her, continuance of the da Silva line is an obsession, and I thought that I, too, could go along with it. But I don't need your money, Camilla, and I shall have no regrets for letting this tainted line die out. I knew, as soon as I first saw you, so fresh and spirited and lovely, that I could not use you in that way, so cynically, as if your part it in was unimportant. I should have sent you home, there and then. I'm sorry. It seems inadequate, but what else can I say?'

He sat down, rested his elbows on the table, and let his head sink into his hands, as if the stress of the long pretence, and the harrowing nature of what he had been obliged to tell her had finally proved too much for him to bear. Seeing him like that, with the proud dark head bent, abject and disconsolate, Camilla's whole being was irradiated by an awareness of love, tenderness and compassion such as she had never known. The force of this was so overwhelming, she realised that what she had felt for him before had been compounded of pique, wounded pride and physical desire, the immature wants of an immature girl. This, in all its fullness, was the love of a woman.

Without a second's hesitation, she sprang up and ran round the table, knelt at his side and put both her arms around him.

'Oh, my darling,' she said brokenly.

He suffered her embrace for a moment and then, with careful and deliberate finality, detached her warm body and sheltering arms, and put her away from him.

'Never do that again,' he said, a tortured expression on his face. 'Never. Do you hear me?'

Camilla stood up, slowly.

'Tell me one thing,' she said, 'and then we shall not speak of it again. Tell me only that you could have loved me.'

He looked at her, taking in every detail of the slender form and small, enchanting face—but more, he looked at her as if seeing through these mere superficial qualities to the indomitable spirit and deep capacity for love that lay between them. A smile broke through his sadness.

'I could have loved you,' he said.

'Thank you,' said Camilla. She did not look back as she turned and left the house, running swiftly through the rain, the same way she had come in his arms a few crowded hours before.

CHAPTER
EIGHT

DURING the days that followed, Camilla was kept fully occupied, as they all were, by the fury of the epidemic that raged through the Tamil lines. The sick filled every available bed, they lay on make-shift pallets on the floor, and every day, it seemed, there were fresh cases. It showed no sign of abating, and all work at Ratnagalla had virtually come to a standstill. For the first time since she had arrived the factory was quiet, the machines lay idle.

Down by the river, the Hindu funeral pyres burned every day, and accompanied by small processions the wasted bodies were consigned to the flames. Camilla knew that for the Hindus this was not the end, but only one stage in a cycle of birth and rebirth, and, watching the funeral processions, she could not help but wonder if it were truly so, if one lived many lives which were like brief flickering dreams in an eternal night, endlessly being snuffed out by sleep.

Standing at her side, watching the smoke rise in the distance, Phillip shuddered.

'Makes you feel uneasy, doesn't it? Even though I've lived most of my life in Ceylon I still find something alien and somehow alarming about these people and their customs.'

Camilla merely smiled and shrugged. She did not find this sinister quality which so disturbed her brother-in-law. To her, it was all part of the rich fabric of Ceylonese life, something different and fascinating, and nonetheless valid.

'No more alarming than they must find our burial customs, lowering a body into the ground in a wooden box,' she said.

He looked at her without comprehension, obviously at a loss to understand how anyone could find the Christian burial service strange.

'Being married to Javier has made you almost as odd as he is,' he said. 'You'll be reading those ancient Sanskrit books next. As for me, I've made a decision. If I come out of this alive, I'm going to join the army. Can't brood around here all my life, waiting for something that isn't going to happen.'

Camilla smiled again, this time encouragingly.

'I think that's a splendid idea,' she said. 'And of course you are going to live through it, don't be so gloomy.'

'How do you know? How does any of us know?' he responded morosely. 'We could all be dead before the week is out. I can't be so damn' calm about it as you apparently can. It's as if you don't care, one way or the other.'

'It's simply that I've stopped worrying about it,' she said. 'There's too much to do.'

Between herself and Javier not a word had passed that was not strictly practical and confined to the business in hand, since that day when he had told her the awful truth about his family. He had made no mention of it, and she had kept her promise not to speak of it again. She tried to erase it from her mind, and partly succeeded. While she was caring for the sick she had not a minute to spare, and in the short rest periods she allowed herself she usually fell at once into an exhausted and dreamless sleep.

But sometimes, in a odd moment here and there, she could no longer prevent it all from flooding back. Watching Doña Lucia, purposefully doling out what remained of her cholera mixture, she wondered what it must be like for her to know she carried within herself the seeds of eventual insanity, to feel it encroaching further as the years and months passed, steadily taking over. She thought of Doña Lucia as a young girl, married to a man she adored, who had taken her for her money, along with the dangers inherent in her. Watching her children as they grew to adulthood, waiting in dread to see where the dark thread would surface yet again.

The Ballantyne wildness and the incipient madness of the da Silvas, a potent and explosive combination. Camilla knew that if Javier would give her the chance, she, too, would accept that risk gladly, even knowing all the facts. But she knew, also, that he would not.

'I am not prepared to give you a child who might inherit this terrible and incurable condition,' he had said. In this, she knew, he was thinking of her, and she had to accept it. Their marriage was over.

There was a little comfort to be derived from knowing that if there had not been this shadow hanging over him, love might have blossomed between them. But it was a bleak little consolation, she knew. Would it be enough to warm all her days and nights that were to come? Would it not be kinder if the cholera simply took her, also, as it had taken so many? There was a death-wish quality about Camilla's unsparing devotion to Ratnagalla's sick workers, but death was not a willing accomplice one could summon as one wished. Camilla's patients continued to die, and she remained untouched.

In the face of so much squalid and painful suffering, Camilla, insouciantly courting death, was able to remain calm. Doña Lucia also maintained a stoical, almost frozen self-control. It was Mohini who finally broke.

After days of imperturbable composure, when she seemed buoyed up by a resolute faith Camilla was compelled to admire, one day she dropped a bowl of water she had been carrying to someone's bedside, and it was as if the accident, trivial in itself, released a hidden spring inside her.

She stood still, unable to move, whilst she crumpled inwardly, and tears ran down the smooth, golden face. Her hands endlessly clasping and unclasping, she sobbed as if her heart would break.

Camilla put an arm around the slim shoulders.

'Don't worry about it. It's only a little spilled water. We are all tired and we all drop things from time to time.'

The girl did not rally as expected. She began to weep noisily, her head in her hands, her body shaking.

Doña Lucia motioned to one of the Tamil women, who, by reason of their own children's sickness, had been conscripted as helpers to clear up the mess.

'Get her out of here,' she said sharply to Camilla. 'I can manage for a while. Get her out, and don't bring her back until she has calmed down.'

Camilla had no time to reflect on her mother-in-law's somewhat uncharitable reaction to outbreaks of hysteria in others. Taking Mohini by the arm, she led her gently outside on to the long verandah.

The Indian girl sank to the ground in a heap.

'I can't bear it any more!' she whispered. 'I never wanted this to happen, never! You must believe me!'

It was an odd choice of words. Camilla sat down at Mohini's side and said, 'But of course you didn't. No one wanted it. It's what it known as an act of God.'

Mohini's dark head jerked upright, and the large, deeply-fringed eyes were wide.

'But the gods do not act in isolation,' she said. 'Sometimes they must be summoned. And there are those who have that power.'

Camilla shivered.

'What you are talking about is . . . is witchcraft, Mohini, a knowledge of and an ability to manipulate occult forces. Who, here, has that capacity to influence events?'

Mohini was almost calm now, only her breathing was still uneven.

'I have,' she said. 'Or at least, I *think* I must have. But I did not bring this about. I did not!'

Camilla stared at her, convinced that the girl must have temporarily taken leave of her senses.

'Oh, come now,' she said. 'You are overwrought and imagining things. I know you, don't forget. You have been my maid these last few months. Is it possible you could have been involved in anything so sinister without my knowledge?'

'You only think you know me,' Mohini said sadly. 'The part of me that I have most wished, and striven hardest to become, that is what you know, and I wish it were all. Oh, I wish more than anything that it were all,' she repeated, and as Camilla continued to regard her with disbelief, she asked suddenly and disconcertingly, 'Did they ever tell you how Edgar Ballantyne died?'

'Yes—' Camilla said hesitantly. 'That is, I gather no one really knew. He was simply found dead one morning, and a satisfactory explanation has never been found.'

'I killed him,' Mohini said flatly.

'You?' Camilla gave a sharp little laugh, despite the gravity of the subject. 'Mohini, you know you could not hurt a fly, so how could you kill a grown man, especially without anyone knowing how you had done it?'

'But that's the whole point, I did not *have* to do anything!' Mohini cried, desperate to be believed. 'You are right, I have a horror of physical violence, and could not lift a finger against anyone. I simply wished him dead, you see. And he died.'

She saw Camilla looking at her with the same unshaken refusal to take anything she had said seriously, and she said, 'You don't believe me, do you?'

'Not for a minute,' Camilla agreed tranquilly. 'I think all this—' her hand encompassed the hospital shed and all the suffering contained within it—'all this has been too much for you, and for that you cannot be blamed. I think, furthermore, you should consider yourself relieved of all duties for the rest of the day, take a sedative and lie down.'

Mohini shook her head stubbornly.

'I *did* kill him,' she said. 'He paid for my education, and I should have been forever grateful. I was deeply indebted to him, but when I came back from Colombo, in my European dress and hairstyle, my head bursting with knowledge, he looked at me, and all he saw was another native girl. All that I had learned was wasted. I wanted to start a school for the Tamil children here, teach them to read and write, and tell them about the Christian God, but Ballantyne sahib would have none of that. The Tamils had a rich culture of their own, he said, and did not need introducing to ours. One educated native girl was sufficient, he did not want the seeds of dissension sown throughout the estate. I could work in the kitchen with my father, he said, there was much for me to learn there.'

Camilla listened to this diatribe with a growing sense of injustice, and mentally she inveighed against her unknown father-in-law for daring to experiment with this girl's life. He should have taken her all the way, or left her alone, it was criminal to have left her thus, suspended between two ways of life, equally valid and mutually contradictory.

'You should have spoken to me about the school,' she said. 'Up to a point, I agree with Edgar Ballantyne about too much proselytising, but literacy can do nothing but good. However, given that you had a grudge against him, not without reason, I still do not accept that you killed him.'

'I wished him dead,' Mohini repeated insistently, 'and he died.'

'You felt guilty because in an angry moment you wished for it, and it came about. That does not make you responsible.'

'Does it not? And how do you think Fanny died?' Mohini asked softly.

'Fanny?' Camilla exclaimed, startled. 'What has Fanny to do with this? She liked you, and I thought you liked her. You will be telling me next you were responsible for her death, also.'

'I was,' said Mohini. 'Of course I was. Yes, I liked her, but I was envious of her favoured position as your maid. On your wedding morning, remember, she said I would make a good lady's maid, and I thought, why not? If only *she* were not there, if only something would happen to remove her, so that I could take her place.'

Camilla was suddenly quiet, remembering all too well that morning, the little cameo of the three of them in her bedroom. She in her bridal gown, Fanny adroitly arranging her hair, and Mohini looking on, with who knew what thoughts forming behind her smooth, impassive face.

But no, it could not be, it was all too ridiculous. She could not and would not accept that there was any connection between these two mysterious deaths and the well-hidden resentment of a girl she had not known so well as she had thought.

'You are distraught and don't know what you are saying,' she told the girl firmly. 'I insist that you take some rest, and then you will see things in perspective again.'

Mohini's velvet eyes glittered with anger, an emotion Camilla had never seen in them before.

'I see clearly enough. It is you who do not,' she cried. 'I have carried this burden for too long. You want to believe that it is all coincidence, these two people dying so unexpectedly and without explanation, because that is part of your calm, rational English upbringing. You will not accept the mystery—even though I know you have felt it, even though its wings brushed by you in the Tamil city.'

Now Camilla was gazing at the other girl with growing alarm and foreboding.

'How do you know about what happened there, that night?' she asked. 'Did you follow me?'

'No,' Mohini said softly. 'I was there before you. You and I were both there.'

An insidious coldness crept up Camilla's spine, spreading out and taking possession of her arms and hands, making the flesh at the nape of her neck creep, and her head throb.

'It was you,' she said, and there was no accusation in her voice, only a new and greater understanding, as when a curtain parts and allows one to see what was previously hidden. 'You were the dancer. I thought it was Anula. But how could I have been so deceived?'

For answer, Mohini reached up and released the heavy veil of her hair from its clasp, and, free from its severe, restraining style, allowed it to float loose in a black cloud around her face. Her expression was transformed, her eyebrows arched, her mouth curved into a complacently sensuous smile. A supple flick of her wrists, a twist of her slim body, completed the metamorphosis, even in her prim, dark serge dress, into the ravishingly voluptuous creature who had danced before the temple of Shiva.

'You see?' she said, still smiling, as if this made immediate sense of everything she had said previously. 'Of course, you only saw me at night, and at a distance, and you expected it to be Anula, because that was what I had led you to believe. If you were fooled, so were the Tamil labourers, because it was always me they saw. Anula never danced at the temple. So far as I know, after the Hindu priest left, she never went near the place. She had no feeling for the dance, or for the rites. Her only interest was in using her body to get what she wanted from men.' Mohini's voice hovered between resentment and contempt. 'I hated her. So I sent her away.'

'You sent her away?' Camilla repeated faintly. 'Javier sent her away. He told me so.'

Mohini shrugged.

'It is all the same. I wanted her gone, and she went.'

'But why? How had she harmed you that you should hate her?' Camilla demanded breathlessly.

'You do not know? Still, you do not know? Mohini was incredulous. 'I hated her because she was nothing but an ignorant, amoral, unscrupulous Tamil whore, and yet she had what I, for all my education, for all the so-called sophistication I had acquired in Colombo, could never hope to possess . . . She had the man I loved. Yes.' She smiled ruefully as Camilla drew in a sharp breath. 'Your husband. I adored him, even when I was a small girl, and when I came back, I loved him more than ever. But he hardly noticed me. *She* had him. And after she had gone, you came, and still he was not mine!'

She was crying again now, tears streaming unhindered down her lovely face.

'There was nothing I could do to make him look at me with seeing eyes. The power I had seemed capable only of destroying. But I never sought to hurt him, or you. I loved you, can you understand that? even while I hated you for taking him from me, yet again.'

Camilla put an arm around the girl's shoulders.

'I understand better than you think, that one can love and hate at the same time,' she said soberly.

'You are not angry?' Mohini said unbelievingly.

'With you? Why? Because you love Javier? How can I blame you for that? I loved him myself, almost as soon as I set eyes on him.'

'But I had no right to,' said Mohini wretchedly.

'Who has rights where love is concerned? Listen to me, Mohini. You are punishing yourself for events which would have taken place with or without your supposed intervention. We may never know what Fanny and Edgar Ballantyne died of, but in the East many people die thus, and will continue to do so until such time as we understand more about the diseases endemic to the tropics. It is the same with this outbreak of cholera. As for Anula, Javier sent her away because he had had enough of her, and she went, presumably, because she realised it was time for her to move on.'

'No!' Mohini cried. 'You are trying to be kind, but it will not work! How can you close your eyes to the truth, you who have seen the bride of Shiva dancing!'

'Ah, yes.' Camilla gave a tight little smile. 'I was coming to that. You wanted everyone, me included, to believe in Anula's presence. That way, you could dance in the temple without anyone suspecting it was you. And yes, you had power, Mohini, I will not deny it, but I sensed no evil in that power. Each and every one of us has dark forces within us, but we also have a capacity for goodness. I do not believe that the capacity for good in you would permit you to use your power for a malign purpose.'

All the time she was speaking, Camilla had never taken her eyes from the other girl's face, so intent was she on convincing her. Now she said, 'I am going to make it an order that you do no more work today, that you go and rest. When this is all over and things are back to normal we can talk again about your school for the Tamil children. Or if it hurts you too much to stay at Ratnagalla, you can get right away, continue your education elsewhere, and become a qualified teacher. Don't worry about the money, I have more than I know what to do with.'

'You will send me away?' Camilla recognised only too

well the panic which flamed in the other girl's face.

'No, not unless you wish to go. This is your home.' She had almost said, I will take you with me when I am sent away myself, but that was a deep secret, of which this was not yet the time to speak.

The door of the hospital shed flew open, and Dona Lucia appeared.

'What is taking you so long?' she said crossly to Camilla. 'I meant you to give the girl a slap across the face and tell her to pull herself together, not to spend the rest of the afternoon deep in conversation.'

'I am coming,' Camilla said wearily. 'Mohini, you go and rest, and think about what I have said.'

The Indian girl nodded silently. Before their eyes, she withdrew into the fragile carapace of reserve behind which she lived most of her life. The tears and the tempestuous emotion were battened down firmly, and her back was straight and rigid, her head high as she turned and walked away.

'Not reliable,' Doña Lucia muttered under her breath. 'They're all the same. I warned you, didn't I? But you would have her for your personal maid. It doesn't pay you to let them get too close. If you had lived out here for as long as I have, you would realise the truth of what I tried to tell you.'

Camilla smiled politely, sighed, and went back to her nursing. She had long ago learned the futility of arguing with her mother-in-law, and it would be worse than foolish to upset her equilibrium now, with so much to do and Mohini temporarily out of action.

In any event, what had passed between herself and the Indian girl was intended for no other ears, and that was the way it would remain, she was determined. She should have been more astonished by the revelations she had heard today, it should have shocked her that the charismatic dancer in the ruined city was not the mysterious, unknown Anula, but Mohini, the gentle girl who brought her tea, and did her hair, and helped her to dress every day. But there was still that sense of a veil lifting— as if this knowledge had been hidden from her by the flimsiet of gossamer curtains, and she had needed only a little better vision to see it all.

Against the girl's firm conviction that she had brought about the death of two supposedly healthy people simply by the exercise of her will, Camilla's own mind fought resolutely. The strange force which had been all around her on that unforgettable night had its source in the deep vein of pleasure Mohini had tapped within herself, dancing under the moon among the ruins, her indentification with the ancient Hindu beliefs and practices despite her westernised education and her ostensible conversion. She doubted that the girl could summon it up in the cold light of day, and direct it against another human being.

For her, quite the strangest thing of all was the discovery that Mohini loved Javier, and always had. The effort it must have cost the girl not to betray this hopeless, lifelong adoration must have been tremendous, for she had never spoken of him aside from a polite, passing reference to 'the master', her eyes had not followed him, and in his presence, she had been demure and restrained.

Only once had Camilla been aware that he had the power to disconcert her, on the occasion when he had quoted the Sanskrit prayer, and Mohini had rushed headlong from the room, and even then, she had mistaken the cause of the girl's distress, as had Javier, who must have been supremely unaware of her passion for him.

Perhaps if she had been less emotionally tied up in her own reactions to him, Camilla thought, she might have been able to interpret the signs correctly. On the whole, she had taken Mohini at face value. For all she had loved the girl, she had only glimpsed, and not heeded, the depths that stirred beneath the smooth surface of the pond. Now she knew everything she was even more determined to do what she could for her.

That day, for the first time in a week, there were no deaths from cholera at Ratnagalla. Camilla slept better, and allowed herself to sleep longer than she had dared since the outbreak began, and prayed that they might be over the worst. In the morning, she found that this hopeful state of affairs had continued. Patients were recovering and being allowed to leave the isolation of the hospital shed and return to their quarters. Some of those still hospitalised were stabilising and had every hope of recovery.

Even the rain was falling less heavily. Once again, there were pluckers out in the fields, and men and machines at work in the factory, although the labour force was sadly depleted. Kanganies would shortly have to make the journey to the poor villages of southern India to recruit fresh workers for the estate.

Only one thing puzzled Camilla on this morning when everything had begun to look so much better. Mohini was absent from the hospital shed. Thinking that she must have been exhausted and overslept, Camilla asked Phillip to go up to the house and get a maid to knock on the girl's door in an attempt to rouse her.

He was back in a short time, alone.

'She isn't there,' he reported. 'I did as you asked, sent a maid up, and she knocked long and hard, but didn't get any answer. Finally, she opened the door and looked in. Mohini was not there, and her bed did not appear to have been slept in.'

'But where could she be?' Camilla said, worried and puzzled. 'Did you see if she was with Lal by any chance?'

'I thought of that. Lal hasn't seen her since early yesterday,' Phillip said.

'Then ask around. Someone must have seen her,' Camilla insisted. Phillip shrugged and went to do as he was bidden, but all his enquiries met with no success. The answer was invariably the same. No one had seen Mohini. The girl had simply vanished.

Camilla pushed back a lock of hair which had fallen across her face. By now, she was more than a little anxious.

'She can't just have disappeared,' she protested. 'Where would she go? We must have some men organised to search for her, scour the estate.'

Phillip backed off, shaking his head.

'Oh no! I'm not going to be the one to give the order! The labour force is below strength as it is, and Javier is not going to relish sparing able-bodied men to search for one missing native girl with too high an opinion of herself.'

Camilla pinned up the straying hair impatiently, shook out her skirts and straightened her back.

'We shall see about that!' she said determinedly, and marched off in the direction of the factory.

The clatter of the machinery presided over by Mac did not disturb Camilla, since she had worked so many days with its noise as an intermittent background, and the men busy with the sorting and firing routine all had a smile for the new young mistress who had not been afraid to soil her hands in the sick room. She walked swiftly through the factory to the office, where she found her husband.

'Good morning, Camilla.' His smile was a query. 'What brings you here? I thought things had taken a turn for the better.'

'They have, so far as the cholera is concerned,' she agreed. 'There were no deaths last night, and no new cases yet, today. But we have another problem. Mohini is missing.'

'Missing? You mean you haven't seen her yet this morning?' he frowned, as if this were not really sufficient cause for disturbing him.

'I mean she is not in her room, her bed has not been slept in, and no one, Lal included, has seen her since yesterday.'

'I see. That does sound rather more serious,' he agreed. 'I gather you want a search party organised?'

She smiled with immense gratitude, relieved and incredulous. Phillip had intimated that she was asking too much, and in the past, she too would have been afraid to ask for such a favour, but it had been so easy.

'Oh, would you? I know you are short of men, but I'm so worried about her!'

He raised a hand to silence her effusive thanks.

'I am not an ogre, Camilla,' he said. 'How could I refuse, after you have looked after these people with such devotion? I know how much that girl means to you.'

His kindness almost broke her heart. She wanted to fling her arms around his neck, but remembered sadly that he had forbidden her to do any such thing. Had she but known it, the relief in her eyes was thanks enough.

All through the morning, the party of men searched, and well into the afternoon, but after each foray in different directions they returned to report that they had met with no success. Ratnagalla was vast, but it did not seem possible that one slip of a girl could get very far, given the weather, and the conditions underfoot. Mohini had disappeared without trace.

Camilla was frantic.

'We have to find her today,' she said. 'Soon it will be dark again, and if we wait until tomorrow . . .'

Javier looked intently at her anxious face.

'There's something you are not telling me,' he said. 'Some reason why she might have taken off as she did.'

Camilla looked at the ground. She could not tell him that Mohini loved him, that she was the one who danced naked before the Hindu temple, that she had got it into her head she was responsible for the deaths of Fanny and his father. These were things she had promised herself never to reveal to anyone.

She said, 'Yesterday, Mohini was distressed and emotional. Everyone has a breaking point, and I think she had reached hers. I sent her off duty for the rest of the day, but foolishly, perhaps, I did not check if she had obeyed me.'

'Why should you have?' he asked gently. 'Don't blame yourself. You, too, are tired and overwrought. It has taken a toll of all our nerves. But let us stop for a minute and think, instead of rushing blindly around, sending people looking here and there without any proper plan of action. Where would she go if she was troubled and in need of help or reassurance?'

Camilla's questioning eyes sought his, and he went on, as if picking a pathway through his thoughts, in an endeavour to understand how someone else's mental processes might work.

'If I feel beset by problems and anxieties, I ride up to the top of the pass, where I can look out over Ratnagalla and see Adam's Peak in the distance. It's as good as a powerful drug for me. Phillip, now, he gets a gun and goes out hunting something. My mother retires to her chapel.' He stopped, as the thought struck him. 'Mohini is religious, isn't she? But there's no church for her to seek sanctuary in.'

Camilla's hands gripped the arms of her chair.

'What a blind idiot I have been!' she exclaimed. 'Of course—where else would she go? And why didn't I think of it, I, of all people? The ruined Tamil city.'

Javier frowned. 'Now why, in heaven's name, would she go there?' he demanded.

'Because,' she replied, 'as you once said, her roots are deeper than she will admit. That's where she is, Javier, I'm sure of it, and that's why she hasn't been found, because it would not occur to anyone to look there.'

He stood up at once.

'If you are really so certain,' he said, 'then it must be investigated. As you say, it will be dark soon.' He paused. 'I think it would be best if I don't send Tamil workers out there to look for her. If the place draws her so strongly that she visits it alone, she might not welcome their speculation about her motives. I'll go myself.'

Camilla was thankful for his tactful approach, but she, too, jumped to her feet and said, 'Very well. I am going with you.'

'That isn't advisable. It will be difficult enough riding, with conditions as bad as they are, without my having to look out for you.'

'I won't impede you, I promise. I know what the terrain is like, I've been there before.' Camilla was adamant. 'Please, Javier. I have to go. I feel responsible for her. This will be the last thing I shall ever ask of you, so don't refuse me.'

He considered her words with the utmost gravity, and said, 'All right. Change into the most weatherproof clothes you have, and I shall have two horses ready for us. But quickly. We can make better time while the daylight lasts.'

In a matter of minutes they were riding out. As Camilla made as if to ride in the direction of the Sinhalese village, Javier checked her.

'No,' he said. 'It's not necessary to go through the village. There's a quicker way, a way used by the Tamils themselves when they visit the temple. Besides, for a few days, until we are sure neither of us has cholera, it would be wiser not to come into contact with any of the villagers.'

Camilla reprimanded herself inwardly for not having thought of this simple precaution, and without a word, urged her horse to follow the path Javier was taking, which cut across the estate and plunged steeply down into the jungle.

As he had warned her, the going was bad, the weeks of

rain had made the ground loose and slippery, and the rampant vegetation even more of a menace. Night began to close swiftly around them as they made their way through the jungle, the last rays of the sun hardly penetrating the thickness of the treetops. Birds called raucously and small animals chattered, the clamour of the jungle awakening at the hour of darkness.

Javier dismounted, tethered the horses, and helped Camilla down, and they pressed forward together on foot.

'It is not far, this way,' he encouraged her. 'You can see, even through the thickest jungle, a path has been worn by the passage of so many feet over the years. Give me your hand.'

She did so, glad of his imperturbable presence, the familiarity with which he moved, unafraid, through the darkness, alive with strange sounds. The clearing was upon them before she had expected it, and approaching the ruins from a different angle, it took her a while to orientate herself and identify the various features.

There was no moon visible, only a misty blackness, and drenched by a persistent drizzle the ancient stones were stripped of their romance. This was not a place of enchantment now, it evoked no echoes of splendid civilisations. It was nothing more than a heap of broken masonry, vandalised by the invading jungle. The maidens did not celebrate, and the concupiscent deities did not embrace, of if they did, the rain obliterated them.

Camilla stood, looking around her, seeing no sign of life at all. Then she pointed a little to her right, and a distance of perhaps fifty yards ahead.

'There it is,' she said. 'The temple of Shiva.'

She started forward, stumbling over the cracked paving that had once been the floor of a building, her skirts becoming entangled by clinging creepers which sought to restrain her. Pushing them away impatiently, she almost ran, crying out with frustration at each obstacle which impeded her progress.

Javier caught her up, and his firm, purposeful hands succeeded in arresting her.

'Camilla, no. Let me go first,' he commanded.

'But I must find her!' she protested, trying unsuccessfully to shake him off.

'If she is here, we *shall* find her. What good will it do if you break your ankle in the process?' he said sternly, refusing to let her go.

The misty clouds parted suddenly, allowing a pale and rainwashed moonlight to filter on to the scene. By its light, they could see the temple of Shiva with sudden clarity, and see also, unmistakably, the motionless figure of a woman, stretched out on the ground.

Camilla gave a sharp cry, and releasing her from his fierce grip, Javier sprang forward, his long stride clearing the distance in a matter of seconds. By the time she caught up with him, her breath coming in gasps, her skirt ripped where she had torn it free of encroaching creepers, he was kneeling by the girl's side, her cold hand in his, feeling for a pulse.

Camilla sank down beside him. Mohini was still wearing her plain, dark servant's dress, but her black hair was loose, and both were rain-sodden. Her eyes were closed, and she was as still as the carved statues on the columns of the temple.

'We must get her home as quickly as possible,' Camilla said urgently. 'I'll take off my cape and we can wrap her in it.'

Javier's expression silenced her anxious chatter.

'My dear, it would do no good,' he said gently. 'She's dead.'

He turned the girl's head slightly to one side, and they saw an ugly gash between temple and ear, half-hidden by the tangled mass of wet hair. 'The paving stones are cracked and uneven, and slippery from the rain. She must have fallen and struck her head.'

Camilla took the girl's body in her arms, and rocked to and fro in unbearable anguish. If she had realised sooner where to look for her, if she had checked that Mohini had gone to her room when she absolved her from duty, if, instead of sending her back to the house, she had made her pull herself together and get back to work—so many irreversible 'ifs' which had led to this young life ending here, amid the uncaring stones and the rain-soaked jungle.

She did not know how long she sat there, nursing the girl's cold body, her tears falling and mingling with the rain. It could not really have been very long before Javier, who had moved away and left her with her very private grief, returned and laid a hand on her shoulder.

'Camilla,' he said quietly. 'Come, now. Let us take her back to Ratnagalla.'

He bent and picked Mohini up in his arms and carried her back to where they had left the horses. How happy the girl would have been in life, Camilla thought, to be held close to him like that. Now there was no more pain of loving without return, no more wondering who she truly was, no more anguished searching of her soul. Mohini was brought back to Ratnagalla, carefully strapped on to Javier's horse, which he led, walking all the way, with Camilla riding behind.

As the small procession made its way up through the lines, the Tamil workers came out on their long verandahs and watched in silence. It seemed to Camilla that no one spoke, but the knowledge of the catastrophe communicated itself, running ahead of them, so that as they approached the house, even the indoor servants crept out covertly to witness their arrival. Last of all came Lal.

He did not shed a tear as he received the body of his daughter, his lean, reserved face remained, as ever, grave and dignified. But the thin, spare shoulders drooped, and all at once he was an old man. The picture of him, standing there with the dead girl in his arms, saying not a word, blaming no one, asking nothing, was etched on Camilla's mind forever.

She slipped from the saddle and went to him, quickly.

'I am sorry,' she said quietly. 'I promised to look after her, and I failed you. The shame is mine.'

He shook his head.

'It was her karma,' he said, with immense resignation. 'It was written on the day she turned her back on this house and the ways of her own people.'

If only, Camilla thought sadly, having turned her back, Mohini had kept it resolutely turned. Her tragedy was that she had been unable to resist glancing over her shoulder. But if, in life, she had been torn between two ways, in death she was given no choice. Lal claimed his daughter back completely, and the following day, the funeral pyre burnt once more beside the river.

'And I still don't know,' Camilla tormented herself, 'whether that is what she would have wanted.'

Javier looked darkly at her.

'It is no longer a matter of what *she* wanted, or of what *you* want. Rather, it is Lal's wishes that count. He is alive, and we have to respect his decision. He is her father, and he has chosen for her. Furthermore,' he added bitterly, 'I can say very little about this matter, for the simple reason that I am in ignorance about it. You alone know the truth about what led that girl to her death in the ruins, and as usual, you do not see fit to enlighten me.'

Still shocked and sick at heart, Camilla turned on him, angrily.

'These are secrets which are not mine to tell you, and therefore I should not do so, even if we were to live together until we were ninety,' she flashed.

'Then it is as well we shall not be living together, since

I do not care to have a wife who keeps secrets from me,'
he said coldly.

Camilla was stung by the icy arrogance of his tone, and
the closed, hard expression which made no allowance
for her own suffering. Where was the firm reassurance
which had supported her in their trek through the jungle, the gentle compassion he had shown her when they
discovered Mohini's body?

'You never cared to have me for your wife at all,' she
said. 'If the cholera patients are sufficiently recovered to
manage without me, and the route to Nuwara Eliya is
passable, I should be glad to leave.'

He surveyed her with the same dispassionate coldness.

'You'll stay, Camilla, until sufficient time has elapsed
for me to be sure you are in no danger of having cholera,
or transmitting it to others. I have chests full of tea in the
factory waiting to be despatched, and even they will not
leave Ratnagalla until I am sure the muleteers are not
carrying the disease.'

'I am not a crate of tea!' she said stormily. 'I am a
human being!'

'Then behave like one,' he said curtly. 'Believe me, I
share your anxiety to be free of this charade we are
trapped in, but for the moment, there are other considerations which are more important.'

CHAPTER
NINE

IT was fortunate that Camilla did not have a great deal of leisure to reflect on his unkindness. Although the patients were much recovered, they still needed a certain amount of care, and that morning, Doña Lucia finally succumbed to fatigue and declared that she must either go to her room and lie down, or collapse on the spot.

'I am no longer so young as I was,' she excused herself. 'At twenty, one can stand sleepless nights and constant running about, at fifty, it is not so easy.'

Looking at her mother-in-law, Camilla saw that her face was grey with tiredness, and the once erect shoulders were beginning to sag.

'You have already done far too much,' she said. 'Please go and rest. I can manage here. They are all on the mend.'

In the evening, only Camilla and Phillip sat down to dinner. Doña Lucia was not hungry and remained in her room, resting. Of Javier there was no sign at all, and Lal informed them that a tray of food had been taken across to the office.

Camilla wondered if her husband was deliberately avoiding her. She knew that now the fury of the monsoon had abated somewhat, allowing the pluckers to get out into the fields, Javier had been out there all hours of the day, riding from one part of the estate to another, exhorting the kanganies to greater efforts, even lending a hand with the plucking himself where they were especially short-handed. Plucking tea in Ceylon was a continuous operation, all through the year the tea bushes were growing, and the young buds had to be picked at the right moment of perfection, or else the fine flavour of the finished product would be impaired. Once darkness had fallen, and it was no longer possible to work in the fields, he was busy in the factory and office, and could not spare the time to come across to the house, change and eat dinner.

Still, she could not help but think perhaps he was glad of this perfectly valid excuse to come into contact with her as little as possible. The time was running out for their mock-marriage, and he must surely feel that the less time they were in one another's company, the better it would be for both of them. She knew he was right, and she should be grateful for his absence. Was it her fault if she ached for the sight of him, even though his only reaction to her was an aloof coldness?

She was glad to retire to her room quite early, and to be alone with her thoughts. She was dull company tonight for Phillip, she knew, and they had found little to say to one another. Before retiring, she had gone to her mother-in-law's room and knocked on the door to enquire if she were feeling better, but Lola had indicated that Doña Lucia was sleeping.

Camilla took a bath, slipped on her robe, and sat in front of her dressing-table mirror, brushing out her hair. She missed Mohini's gentle presence even more than she had expected to. It was hard to believe she would never again see the Indian girl's slim, neat form flitting quietly about her tasks, never share with her the conversation they had both enjoyed.

She sighed, and gazed at her reflection, taking no pleasure in the face that looked back at her. It had gained in maturity and character, but had lost forever its youthful insouciance, there were lines of tiredness around the clear, hazel eyes, and their expression was one of wistful resignation.

A light knock on the door disturbed her thoughts, and

Javier's voice called quietly, 'Camilla? May I come in, just for a moment?'

'Yes, of course,' she replied, making a supreme effort to keep her voice level and unemotional.

He had obviously just come in from the factory, since he had not changed, and looked, if anything, even more fatigued than she did.

Impulsively, she said, 'You should not work so hard. What benefit will it be to Ratnagalla if you wear yourself to a shadow?'

The beginnings of a smile flickered briefly across his face.

'You are right, of course,' he admitted. 'I am going to turn in now. I just called in at the hospital shed to check how things were going, and it appears that for the third day there have been no further cases of cholera.'

'That's true,' she confirmed. 'Does it mean that the outbreak is over—that it's going to be all right?'

'Hopefully,' he said. 'We can't be absolutely sure, but it's beginning to look like it.'

He came and stood behind her, his eyes seeking those of her reflection in the mirror.

'Camilla, I wanted to say I'm sorry for the way I spoke to you this morning. No one has done more than you have at Ratnagalla, since this outbreak began, and God knows, you have reason enough to hate all of us. Knowing the strain you were under, and your grief at Mohini's death, I should not have said what I did. The least I can do is to ask you to forgive me.'

'Gladly,' she said at once. 'I, too, said things that would have been better left unsaid. Please let us forget all about it, and maybe we can part as friends, and remember one another with . . .' she faltered a little, 'with respect and affection.'

'Respect and affection,' he repeated wryly. 'Do you think we can do that, Camilla? Do you think for us that is possible?'

He sat down on the bed, weariness showing in every line of his body, and before she could even formulate an answer, tiredness overcame him. He stretched out his long frame full length on the bed, closed his eyes, and was asleep almost at once.

Camilla stood looking down at him, and a smile hovered around her lips. She bent down and gently eased off his boots, carefully lifted his head and laid a pillow under it. He was too exhausted to be aware of her ministrations, and did not stir at all. Quietly, she extinguished the lamps and sat down on the bed beside him.

There was a painful joy in having him here with her, like this, even though he was not aware of her presence, and she sat there for longer than she knew, listening to his deep, even breathing, sharing with him the only night they had ever spent together.

After a while, her own eyelids began to flutter, and the need for sleep stole over her irresistibly. She lay down next to him and closed her eyes, and a fugitive happiness crept into her heart as she drifted into sleep.

She awoke to a sensation of ineffable sweetness, a touch as light as a butterfly's wing brushing her forehead, moving over her cheek and down to her throat. Still half asleep, she murmured with pleasure at this unknown caress, believing it to be a dream from which she had not the desire to awake. But slowly, she became aware that it was no dream, it was real, and her eyes opened.

It was still night, the only light in the room came from the reluctant moonlight filtering through the half-closed blinds. But there was light enough to see the man raised on one elbow, bending over her, with a look on his face such as she had despaired of ever seeing there, compounded of tenderness and longing and desire, and his was the touch which had disturbed her sleep.

She said nothing. Words were superfluous, his touch, and his eyes, had told her all she needed to know, and imprisoning his hand in hers, she carried it to her lips. They held each other's gaze for a moment, acknowledging silently the mutual desire he had so long denied, but could no longer. And then he drew her close to him, covering her face with kisses, seeking her mouth with intense and determined passion.

Even as she held him in her arms and gave him in return whatever his kisses demanded, she knew that he had not meant this to happen, had not intended that featherlight caress to wake her, so that she might surprise on his face the need he had so assiduously suppressed. But the proximity of those few hours spent together in sleep had created a new and irresistible intimacy between them, so that he could no longer fight both her desire and his own, and the hands that now claimed her could not prevent themselves from asking more, carrying her with him into an overwhelming delight, from which there was no drawing back. Camilla felt the world fall away, as, conversely, he gave it back to her, a hundredfold.

For a long while they lay in each other's arms, content to be still and let the tide of ecstasy recede from them. And when finally she dared to look into his face, she saw that his joy at the ardour of her response was touched with sadness.

'So now you know, my love,' he said, with a regretful smile, brushing her hand with his lips. 'Now I cannot pretend to you any more, cannot say I do not love you, and hide behind my supposed indifference. I love you, Camilla. For whatever it is worth.'

Her eyes brimmed with tears, and she buried her face in his shoulder. The day she had yearned for, for so long, had finally come, after she had renounced all hope of ever hearing him say those words. But although the words were sweet, there was bitterness in his voice.

'It is worth everything to me,' she declared fiercely. 'I have loved you almost from the day we met.'

'And almost from the day we met, I have been fighting against my need to return that love,' he said gravely. 'I knew at once—how could I not know—that you were the woman I was destined to love, and I knew that I must resist it, that I must not give way to the temptation. Every minute we were alone together, I wanted to take you in my arms. I fought it the only way I could, by avoiding those occasions when we might be alone, by refusing to acknowledge any kind of rapport between us. And—forgive me, my dearest—by being, at times, as hateful to you as I possibly could.

'Even then, there were moments when your beauty, and your spirit broke through my defences, times when I had to hurt you to remain in control. And when I caught Phillip attempting to seduce you, I went out of my mind with jealousy.'

Camilla turned in his arms.

'My darling, no one can fight against love as strong as this,' she told him. 'Haven't we just proved that, beyond all doubt?'

'All we have proved is that I am weaker than I realised,' he said bitterly. 'You looked so beautiful and vulnerable lying there asleep, that I had to touch you, just once. I thought you would never know, but when you awoke and looked at me, I was overcome by the need to make love to you. I gave in, and I am deeply ashamed. If I could wipe out the last half hour I would gladly do so.'

'But I would not,' she said. 'Those were the most wonderful minutes of my life.'

'Of mine, also,' he confessed. 'But I have ruined you in those minutes, dearest. Now it will be impossible for us to get an anulment on the grounds that the marriage did not exist, and without that, you can never be free to find someone who can give you a normal life.'

'You still want to send me away,' she murmured, 'after all that we have been to one another?'

'I have to,' he said wretchedly. 'This has changed nothing, Camilla, except that we now know, to our cost, what we are losing. I cannot live with you, wondering each time we make love whether I have given you a child who carries that fatal sickness. As I am wondering now, Camilla, at this very moment.'

She smiled into the semi-darkness. Not for a second did she underestimate the torment he was going through, but because he was a man she could not hope to make him understand the way a woman feels about the unborn child of the man she loves. He saw it only as a disease he might wrongly inflict on her, a danger to which he had no right to subject her. But if, as a result of this ecstatic interlude, she had conceived his child, she would bring it into the world and cherish it, no matter what. She was not afraid.

She put her arms round him and held him close, feeling the strength of his heartbeat, and the urgency of desire quickening their bodies again.

'Maybe it is already too late,' she said serenely. 'I don't care about tomorrow, Javier, nor do I care about the future. All I ask of you is—give me this night.'

Dawn was already flushing the sky when they fell asleep, and the night they had given each other, minute by minute, was almost over. Whatever happened, Camilla thought with perfect tranquillity, as she laid her head on his shoulder and closed her eyes, she could face it with courage. If he asked her to leave she would do so, without argument or reproach. For what had passed between them tonight, she was every bit as responsible as he, and was prepared to bear that responsibilty. She would accept his decision, and not abuse the memory of this night by using it as a weapon with which to blackmail him into letting her stay.

As for annulment, divorce, or eventual remarriage to anyone else, all these notions she tossed aside with a fine contempt. She loved him and knew that he loved her, and wherever she went, even if they agreed never to meet again, that would always be so, and could never be taken from her. Almost as if, on the verge of sleep, the same thought had crossed his mind, the arm that cradled her tightened instinctively, and his hand closed possessively around hers.

A frantic knocking on the bedroom door roused them to sudden wakefulness not long after. Camilla sat up and called out, 'Yes? Who is it?' still bemused by sleep.

'It is Lola . . . please, I must speak with you!' the woman's voice cried urgently.

Camilla struggled into her robe, went to the door and opened it a little. Not that there ought to have been anything unusual about her husband sharing her bedroom, but Camilla was virtually a bride this morning, and was reluctant for Lola to see the rumpled bed, and Javier stretched out near-naked on it.

Lola, however, was far too anxious to give any thought to how the occupants of the room had spent the night.

'It is the mistress!' she cried, distraught and tearful. 'Very sick! Since yesterday. She say to tell no one, and for the first time in my life I disobey her! Please come!'

Even the sight of the master, wearing only a sheet knotted around his waist for decency's sake, which might have given the elderly spinster an attack of apoplexy on any other occasion, scarcely perturbed her this morning.

'What is the matter with my mother, Lola?' he demanded authoritatively.

'Much sickness, sir, and very high fever. Also, pain in the stomach. Sir, I am afraid she has the cholera!'

Camilla looked at Javier, and saw the muscles around his jaw tighten.

'Go back and stay with her,' he ordered quietly. 'Try to keep calm. We shall be with you in five minutes.'

They dressed swiftly, with no time for lingering over

each other, no thought for anything but the new crisis which was upon them. Javier fastened Camilla's dress with practised ease, and she caught back her hair and tied it in a knot at the nape of her neck.

'Why would she refuse to let Lola tell anyone she was ill?' Camilla whispered, as they hurried along the corridor.

'Because she is a stubborn and self-willed woman, and took it into her head to die alone,' he replied grimly.

Doña Lucia's bedroom was in half-darkness, as it so often was, but to Javier and Camilla, with the memories of the hospital shed fresh in their minds, the unmistakable stench of the room left them in no doubt. Her pain-racked face and body burning with fever confirmed their fears. It was cholera—just when they thought it was over, it had struck yet again, and this time, in the big house itself.

'I did not send for you,' Doña Lucia said, clutching her abdomen as another spasm of pain siezed her. 'Lola, how dare you go explicitly against my orders?'

'Lola did the right thing. She has always done what was best for you, and you must not rebuke her for it,' Javier said gently, laying a hand on his mother's forehead. 'It was foolish of you to hide from us the fact that you were sick. You have given the disease a day's start, and made our work in fighting it harder. However, that cannot now be helped. Lola—fetch the cholera mixture, and some boiled water.'

Camilla persuaded her mother-in-law to drink a little of the boiled water. She knew all too well that the best hope for anyone with this sickness was to combat the process of dehydration from the very beginning. But Doña Lucia, by keeping to herself the fact that she was ill for almost twenty-four hours, had prevented them from taking this action. And when she tried to give her some of the mixture, she turned her head away and refused to touch it.

'You are . . . wasting your time,' she forced out the words between the spasms of agonising cramp, which were already attacking her muscles. 'It is too late.'

Camilla looked helplessly at Javier.

'What can we do?' she whispered. 'She won't let us help her at all. Can you get through to Dr Davies in Nuwara Eliya?'

Doña Lucia must have heard what she said, for she shook her head feebly.

'You are a good girl, Camilla, but you must know the doctor can do nothing else for this. There is no treatment other than what we have applied ourselves, these last weeks. And it would be . . . wrong to risk spreading the infection . . . keep it at Ratnagalla.'

Her voice trailed off and Javier knelt by the bed and took her hand, speaking as persuasively as he could.

'But won't you let us help you, mother? We can fight this only if you fight with us.'

'For what?' she flared at him, with a sudden burst of strength. 'So that I can die in a strait-jacket, like my mother did? Is that what you want for me, Javier?'

He was silent for a while, still holding the feverish hand, and Camilla could sense the struggle going on inside him. Finally, he shook his head.

'No,' he said quietly, and with resignation. 'No, that is not what I want.'

'Then let me go!' she whispered fiercely. 'This is a merciful adversary, and I shall not fight it. I see the hand of God in it, my son.'

Her fingers tightened over his, and he smiled a little.

'I see an obstinate woman who will have it her own way,' he said.

Throughout the day, Camilla remained with the sick woman, tending her just as she had looked after the Tamil labourers, for in the extremity of illness, all were equal. But there was a subtle difference, for now she was not nursing a patient fighting grimly and tenaciously for life, but one who had made up her mind to die, and now she saw how powerful the human will must be, for unresisted, the disease ravaged Doña Lucia's body with a terrible swiftness.

'At this rate, she will not last the night,' she whispered to Javier in the corridor. Doña Lucia had long since ordered both her sons from the sickroom, saying that she did not want men witnessing her indignity.

Phillip left speedily and with some relief, and contented himself with pacing up and down the hall at the bottom of the stairs, with occasional recourse to the brandy bottle. Javier took up his station on a chair outside the door, and no one saw the *Periya Durai* in the fields that day. Word spread quickly around the estate that the mistress was dying, and an awesome hush pervaded the atmosphere of the house.

As night fell again, Camilla perceived that her mother-in-law was entering the final stage of the disease. The vomiting had ceased, her temperature dropped, her pulse was low and her hands and feet were deathly cold. But she was fully conscious and in complete possession of her faculties, as if the approach of death had cleared all confusion from her mind. She sent for Phillip, and Camilla left them alone for a while. What words passed between them, she never knew, but the young man looked choked and in a daze as he emerged.

'I can't believe it,' he said. 'How can she simply let herself die like this? She won't even let me fetch the priest, even though she has been a practising Catholic all her life. Says we must isolate the infection. Do you think her mind has finally given way?'

'Absolutely not,' Camilla said firmly. 'She is quite lucid and perfectly clear as to what she is doing. Your mother is facing death with sanity and courage.'

'If there's nothing I can do, I shall be downstairs in the drawing-room,' he said, with a helpless shrug. 'She wants you both to go in, now.'

Doña Lucia dismissed the weeping Lola from the room with a slight gesture of her hand which clearly cost her a great deal of effort. Camilla and Javier sat one at either side of her bed, and she looked at each of them in turn.

'You know,' she said, her voice parched and dry, 'that I have only one wish left unfulfilled, and that is for you two to have a child.' Her searching gaze studied Camilla's pale face. 'I should die happy if you were to tell me that my wish was about to be granted.'

The girl looked down. She could not look into the face of this woman, so close to death, and swear that she was carrying a child. At best it would only be a wild guess, at worst a downright lie, and Doña Lucia's senses were sharpened to the point where it would be impossible to deceive her.

'I cannot say,' she faltered.

Across the bed, her eyes met Javier's, and in them, she read all the abhorrence that the mere possibility aroused in him, the dread that he was unable to hide. Almost imperceptibly, she shook her head, trying to warn him to mask that too obvious repugnance so that his mother should not see it, but it was too late.

'Javier,' she said urgently, 'who will work Ratnagalla after you if you do not have sons? Did your father build up all this so that it could pass to strangers? It is your duty, don't you see?'

Outside, the rain hissed against the windows, in the room, the lamps flickered. The sick woman reached out and gripped the hands of the man at her bedside, willing him to answer, and Camilla wished only that he would consent to what she said, and give her peace. But he, too, seemed to realise that his mother was beyond the point where anything less than total honesty would suffice.

'No, I don't see,' he said bluntly. 'If your loathing of this . . . this malady in our blood is so great that you